COPPER & MERCURY

Copper
and
Mercury

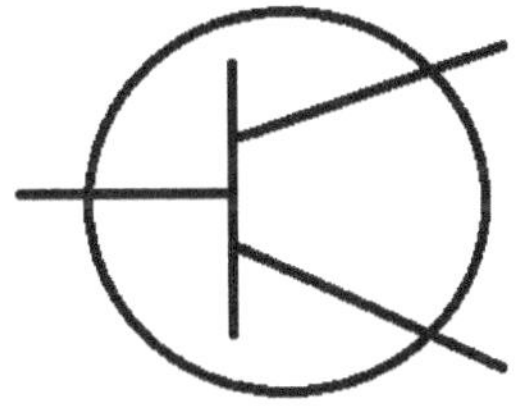

JESSICA D. COPLEN

The Periodic Tales
of Minni the Witch

For

Leaf

&

Potato

ONE[1]

Wednesday, January 31st, 2018
3:01am

Okay, so the building may currently be a smoldering pile of ash, sure, but it was on fire when I got here. And, hey, I put it out: what more do you want from me?

Alright, fine, if you really want to know, this all started earlier this evening. For me at least. I was woken up from a nice dream by my phone going off. My boyfriend sleepily grabbed it, half handing it/half throwing it at me. It was terribly cute.

"Thanks, babe," I mumbled as I tried to focus my eyes on the caller ID. I didn't recognize the number, and it wasn't an area code I was familiar with, either. I swore if this was some robo-call at 9pm, I was going to hunt down whoever thought that was a good idea and fry all their systems.

"Hello?" I answered.

"Minni, it's Phil," he immediately said. "I need you to come bail me out."

"Out of what?" I was not fully awake at that point.

"Jail."

"Huh." For whatever reason I was expecting him to say something a bit more supernatural, you know? A metaphorical bail than an actual bail. "You're in *jail* jail?"

"Yes." He was exasperated and the line crackled.

"You want me to get Ryan?"

"I don't want you to bust me out," he said in a whisper. "The bail is only five hundred dollars. I don't have that on me."

I closed my eyes and almost fell back asleep. "The rent's gone through."

"Minni… it's nine o'clock. Have you already gone to bed?"

"The cat's been fed," I mumbled, despite the fact that neither my boyfriend, nor myself, own a cat.

"Okay, I need you coherent right now." His voice teetered somewhere between anxious and completely done with me. One of these is more normal than the other.

"Alright, one sec." I placed the phone over my chest as I focused. I touched my aura and pulled at the magic, sending energy through my body. It was like a jolt of caffeine. I became energized to the point that I was wide awake. I sat up in bed, running my free hand through my hair as I went back to the phone. "Okay, I'm awake. You got arrested?"

"Yes." Phil was definitely done with me. "I nearly took down their booking computer so I'd like to get out of here before I cause any real damage."

"Tell me what you need me to do."

"Go by the shop," he said as I started to get out of bed. "Ryan knows where I keep the petty cash, there should be enough. You'll need to use the shadow gate near the shop. Use the map, it's like two lefts and a right, to get you to Rome."

"Italy?" I almost squeaked.

"Upstate New York." The connection crackled. "Be as quick as you can."

"I'm on it," I assured him but the phone cut off.

I went to the bathroom and considered taking a quick shower, and now I kind of wish I had. Seeing as I was at Marcel's, I had some clean clothes, though not a large selection. I grabbed yesterday's jeans, but they're jeans, so it's okay. It only took me like five minutes before I was putting on my sneakers.

"You leaving?" Marcel asked, finally joining the land of the living himself.

"Yeah, gotta bail Phil out of jail." I started looking for my coat, having forgotten where I left it.

Marcel rolled over, frowning. "What was he arrested for?"

"I dunno," I admitted because I honestly didn't think to ask. "Can't be all that bad, it's only a five-hundred-dollar bail. And it's Phil."

"Want me to come with?" He's such a sweetheart.

"Nah, you sleep. You have to be up dog ass early," I reminded him. Marcel's doing the early shift this week while one of his coworkers is on vacation. That means a really messed up sleep schedule for him, and for me as I try to be supportive and all that. "No need for you to suffer, too."

I gave him a kiss, grabbed my stuff, and headed out the door. It was hella cold outside because, well, New York... in January. I'm from Nebraska, and I tell you, it's not natural for some place to be so cold, so often, for so long.

Yes, I know how climates work, that's not the point.

Now, I'm really good at controlling energy. It's my special skill. So it's easy for me to create a thermal shield. It keeps me warm in these kinds of conditions. Doesn't stop me from complaining about the cold though. You know, to keep up appearances. I also don't like to use it in front of Marcel because he might get suspicious of how I'm not freezing to death in this weather.

Oh, it had snowed, so that was fun.

I got to the Mercury Shop in decent time. Ryan waited for me at the front. The shop was already closed for the night, so he quickly unlocked the door and let me in.

"What did Phil get arrested for?" he asked as he locked up.

"I dunno." I shrugged and headed towards the back where the shadow gate maps were kept.

"You didn't ask?"

"Didn't seem relevant at the time." Translation: I never ask these things which is why I'm always getting myself into trouble.

"Huh," was Ryan's only comment.

I started sifting through all the ledgers that sat on a bottom shelf. Eventually I found the New York State book, pulling it out from under half a dozen others. With a thud, I sat it on the table and flipped through it to get to the R's.

"Oh, well, great," I said unenthusiastically. "There are two Romes."

"In Italy?"

"No, upstate New York." I pointed at the lines that listed both cities with completely different directions through the shadow realm. Who knew there was two of them?

"Rome, New York?" Ryan quietly questioned before making a sudden, "oh" sound.

"What?" I asked.

"Werewolves."

"Werewolves?"

"Werewolves."

"Ugh, *werewolves*."

"Yeah." Ryan pointed to a Rome. "We need to go there."

"We?"

Ryan grinned. "You think I'm going to miss bailing *Phil* out of jail?"

I chuckled, grabbing a notepad and writing down the directions. "It's cold out, dress accordingly."

"Be right back." Ryan disappeared upstairs and I turned the paper over in my hands.

I wasn't too keen to find out what led Phil to Rome and into a jail cell. I mean, werewolves are decent people. Unlike some other groups, they aren't bent on world domination or have a general kill-all-the-things mentality. The packs just want to be left alone. They're very adamant about that.

So, for Phil to go out of his way, in every literal sense, to deal with them? Let's just say, I had a bad feeling about this.

"Ready." Ryan came bounding down the stairs in hiking boots and about four layers of clothes, complete with a hoodie, coat, and scarf.

"Oh, did you get the money?"

Ryan padded his pocket. "Yeah, we're good."

"Okay then." We let ourselves out the back door, locking up and setting the security ward to full power.

Now, a shadow gate is a fun little rip in reality. I'm sure there is an explanation that involves a lot of physics-speak but, whatever. Just know there are places where our world and the shadow realm touch close enough that it's possible for people to cross between them. Well, it's easier for those in our world to cross into the Shadow Realm than for shadow creatures to cross into ours because, again, physics. Yeah, not a big fan.

I'm an *electrical* engineer. I had to take exactly one physics class, *one*, and it was technically an elective.

Anyway, when Phil was looking for a place to set up shop, he found a building literally a stone's throw away from one of these gates, or rips, tears, whatever you want to call them. The original builders of the area knew about the gate, so they designed the block around it. The back of the buildings lining the alley carried on until there was a small indention in one the structures.

People pass these all the time and don't realize it. It's looks like a small, gloomy, courtyard with a wrought iron fence. But there's no way to get to it from the building, unless you want to climb through a window. So it becomes this slightly overgrown waste of space with random bits of litter that have no business being that far north from the nearest place you can find them.

There was no lock on the gate, because that simply invites people to break in and accidently fall into the Shadow Realm. And of course, if someone comes out of the gate, they don't want to be locked inside the courtyard.

"You ready?" I asked Ryan as we checked to make sure we weren't being watched.

"I'm good."

"'Kay." I took his hand and we walked through the nearly invisible cut in the fabric of reality. In theory, following a path set between the gates was safe, but one could never be too cautious when traveling in groups.

It can be difficult to describe the Shadow Realm, mostly because, like the Earth, it is as wide and varied in its geographical and environmental presentation. It can look like the stuff of nightmares, or Lake Como. It really just depends on who lives in that particular location. Never trust anything from the shadow realm, no matter what it looks like. For here, the beautiful is truly deadly, and the ugly probably just wants to play a good game of Canasta.

This particular section of the realm was a rolling fog bank over a slightly swampy landscape. There was no sun or moon, nothing that gave off an obvious source of light, but I could see about fifty feet in front of me. Ryan in tow, I kept walking for about six minutes until I got to the first left I was to take. It was represented by a sign post made of pig iron dug deep into the ground. It was placed there back in like the 1790s.

We went left, following the marker pointing us towards Shawmut Peninsula. After a few minutes, we took another left towards De-o-Wain-Sta, which is the native name for what you might know as the Oneida Carry. The directions required a bit of back-tracking, but you have to stay in the safe areas, avoid the quicksand as it were.

I stopped suddenly. Ryan bumped into me.

"What?" he asked.

"I thought I heard something." I really did, but it was such a light whisper that I wondered if I had imagined it. Just because you are physically safe on the path doesn't mean creatures can't do their best impression of a siren and try to entice you to walk towards your own doom. "It sounded like…"

Okay, so back in September, there was this guy, Canton, and he, well, he tried to destroy the world, or maybe just Manhattan. He's still in a serious magic-induced coma right now so we can't exactly get that cleared up. Anyway, I had an empathy mergence with some memories he left behind in his old house. I saw him fall through the shadow realm using his grandfather's focus item.

If you have a natural ability to manipulate the folds in reality that allow Shadow Realm travel, then you don't have to take these paths like the plebeians do. The Elder Canton developed a workable travel spell into his focus item, aka his wedding ring, which was then passed down. Canton the younger used the spell on instinct to escape a deadly fire, but his trip through the Shadow Realm wasn't as well controlled as it could have been.

Wouldn't hell be better than this windowless world?

I tried to erase every bit of Canton's memories from my mind, but these words which were spoken to him as he passed through the shadows, they are all that remain. And I could hear them whispered in the fog.

"Minni?" Ryan nudged me because we stopped.

This was the first time I'd used the paths in the Shadow Realm since the incident. It never once occurred to me that the voice would still be there.

"Something to deal with later," I said, pushing us forward.

Yeah, no, I am not dumb enough to walk off the path completely unprepared just to chase down the whisper of a voice. If it was still there now, then it would be there later. And I would be ready for it.

We took a right after about three minutes, walked another six, and we arrived at our destination, another pig iron post. Thankfully Rome, New York, has its own Shadow Gate, which makes travel there pretty swift and easy. Well, aside from the whole trespassing on federal land part.

Back in the mid 1700s, the British built a fort to guard part of a trade route. They positioned it to also guard a Shadow Gate at the same time. They wanted to make sure the natives couldn't use the gates to drive their colonizing assess back to the sea. This one was called Fort Stanwix and it was progressively built-on and abandoned several times over the years. Eventually the National Park Service built a reconstruction of it to serve as a national monument to white history. But they did do an amazingly good job at the restoration, I have to give them props for that.

The higher-ups in the Park Service are well aware of the Shadow Gates which dot a lot of their land. A small, empty building sat atop the tear at Fort Stanwix, guarding it. Ryan and I stepped out into the drafty, wood-log-built room, a dampness in the air from the fresh dust of snow outside.

"Where are we?" Ryan asked.

"Let me check." I pulled out my phone and that's when I learned everything I just said about Fort Stanwix. "Well, not the first protected landmark I've ever trespassed in."

"Try not to set this one on fire," Ryan mumbled as if I make a habit of setting things on fire. I don't, actually. I'm more likely to electrocute than burn. Or use the nearest blunt object.

"Okay, the police station is surprisingly not far from here. Google says a nine-minute walk."

"Or faster if we get ourselves arrested," Ryan mused as he went and checked the door.

"Use your third eye," I told him to do it because I didn't want to. "If whoever built this knows about magic, then there should be a designated path out of the fort, avoiding security."

Ryan blinked a few times, then nodded. "Got it, let's go."

It was dark out, but the was moon full in a clear-ish sky. I easily followed Ryan and saw no glimpse of another soul until we got out onto the street. Mostly it was just a few cars driving past, no one else bearing the cold, wet weather like us two idiots.

The Rome police station was a two-story sorta-red brick building that probably came out of the '70s if I had to guess. There was a large, blocky, transom window over the double-door entrance. A flat roof too, which I honestly don't understand why anyone would ordain to put a flat roof on any building in a place where it actually rains.

Walking inside, the lobby was lined with a couple of chairs and a bench, flyers stuck up on the wall. The rest of the building was blocked by a heavy door. A receptionist sat behind a sheet of ballistic glass like a bank teller.

"How can I help you?" the woman asked in about as monotone voice as one could manage.

"We're here to bail out Phil McCree."

She eyed me for me for a second. "One moment."

The woman disappeared off to her left, the two desks behind her unmanned and the area fairly quiet. I don't imagine a town the size of Rome sees a lot of action on a Tuesday night. Well, when I'm not involved anyway.

There was a click and the side door opened up. A man who had cop written all over him, from his shoes to his belt to the cut of his hair, stepped out. He stopped and sized us up as quickly as I did him. Most people look at me and determine I'm not a threat. I try not to be, but sometimes shit happens.

"I'm Detective Longtree," he introduced himself. "Can I see your ID, ma'am?"

"Ah, sure." I slipped my driver's license from my phone case and handed it over.

He took it, nodded to himself, then passed it back. "I'm handling Mr. McCree's arrest. He said you were some kind of magic sink?"

"I channel energy, so yeah, basically." I'd already reached out and felt Phil's magical signature towards the back of the building. I started siphoning it off without even thinking about it.

"Alright, I'll get him while you fill out some paperwork." He gestured over to the woman at reception who was obviously listening in. "We'll expedite everything."

"Why arrest him in the first place if you're so keen to get him out of here?" Ryan asked, half hiding himself behind me.

"He assaulted a prominent member of the community, in front of witnesses," Longtree explained. "Despite everything you think you know about Rome, a large part of the population is still unaware of werewolves, magic, and the like. Trying to keep it that way is part of our mission statement here at RPD."

"Oh, that's okay then," Ryan agreed as if he was a town council member or something.

"Assaulted someone?" Was what I got stuck on. I figured this had been about some kind of B&E. I mean, Phil isn't a stranger to fighting, you know, when it's a supernatural creature or rogue wizard. But this sounded so... mundane.

"I'll let him fill you in on the details," Longtree said and headed back to the door. "I'll bring Mr. McCree out in a few minutes."

There was a click as the receptionist remotely unlocked the door, the detective disappearing into the back of the station. The woman already had the paperwork filled out for us, which was nice. And they weren't kidding about wanting to expedite things. It was the fastest I've ever had to deal with bailing someone out.

Happens more than you think. I once had to take a shadow gate down to Florida to accompany a local coven leader as they bailed out someone for, let's just say.. `an incident,' cause, you know, *Florida*.

I passed over the bail and heard the main entrance behind me open. I glanced back at the newcomer, because occasionally I do have spatial awareness and self-preservation skills.

"Minni?" the man said as he let the door close behind him. He was tall, his deep red hair cropped closely in a lawyer haircut. The smattering of freckles across his nose made him look a bit younger than he really was. Which is good for a man about to hit his sixties.

"Oh, hey," I said in surprise. "What are you doing here?"

"I heard Phil was arrested," he answered as he shifted his briefcase to his other hand. "I was already in town and thought I'd come by and see if I could help."

"That's nice of you." I mean, there was no reason he had to come, even if he was in the area.

"Who's this?" Ryan whispered at me.

"Oh, sorry, this is Ryan." I pointed Ryan out to the man. "He works for Phil. Ryan, this is my Uncle James."

Now, I very much take after my mother, who's Cheyenne, but my dad, he's about as Irish as one can get. And alright, I'll admit it, I get a little kick out of seeing the varying degrees of double take that people do when I introduce any member of my dad's side of the family. That momentary questioning of reality.

It's a cheap gag, I get it. But it was a good distraction from the memory of the last time I saw Uncle James, which was the first time I met Phil.

And I kind of hated both of them for it.

TWO[2]

March 9th, 2013

Yes, it had rained, but it was the blood of her brother, and his attacker, which soaked the ground, her clothes, even seeping into her socks. Her hands trembled as she cradled her brother's head, having already given him time by using the other man's lifeforce as a temporary reprieve from death.

If she heard the frenzied shouting, she didn't consciously acknowledge it until others came running into the clearing of crushed sunflowers. They stumbled to a stop at the sight before them.

"Minni," her father's voice was in her ear, his hands on hers, trying to extract her from her brother. "Minni, I need you to let go, okay?"

She found herself standing, staring down at David as their sister, the one who was an apprentice healer, got to work. More were coming. Her father slipped the copper focus from her wrist.

"Call your Uncle James," he told Minni's eldest brother as he palmed the bracelet to him. "Tell him to meet us in Lexington."

The man ran off just as more people gathered into the clearing. It didn't take them long to realize what Minni had done. Her father kept his hand on her, protectively. Master healers took away David, casting spells over him even as two men carried him on a stretcher. She could see it on her father's face, the desire to go with David but the sense to stay with her. His son was going to live. The same could not be said of his daughter.

Minni was taken immediately to the Mid-Western Magic Council's satellite office outside Lexington, Nebraska. They placed her in an anti-magic holding cell, shoving her inside as she heard her father demanding to speak to specific members of the council before anything was done. She had no doubt he would do whatever he could to protect her, short of a direct violation of the council's orders. All he had to do was get the council to rule in his favor.

Cut off from her magic, Minni had nothing to do but stare at the blood on her hands, buried in the crevasses of her nails.

The door opened and an apprentice to one of the council members stepped in with a bundle in her hands. It was a change of clothes, seeing as Minni's was stiff, dyed brown by dried blood. Hers. David's. The Attacker's. Minni wordlessly accepted the offering, acknowledging the woman's directions and kindness with a simple nod.

The cell was meant for long term use, if needed, so it came equipped with a shower, the water flowing through copper pipes. It's not that she could see them, but she could feel the copper through the brick. It called out to her as she kept reaching for a copper focus that wasn't there. Her father had been right to take it, to keep the council from it.

There was no mirror. It was far too much of a risk to have in a prison.

Freshly cleaned and dressed in reasonably fitting clothes, she sat down on the small bed. Scooting back, she lifted her knees to herself, wrapping her arms around them as she curled her back. There was no point in worrying or placating anxiety. Whatever was going to happen, would happen, regardless of what she thought about it.

She may have nodded off, but some intangible time later, there was a knock on the door. Less of a request and more of a polite warning that someone was about to enter. Minni glanced up to see her father's brother walk into the room.

"Minni." He tried to smile but this was not an occasion that dictated one.

"Uncle James," she hoarsely replied back.

He frowned at her and checked the water pitcher sitting on the only other large piece of furniture in the room, a desk. Finding the container full, he poured a glass and handed it over to his niece. "Drink. You'll appreciate it later."

Minni accepted the glass, mumbling, "How's David?"

"Depends on who you ask." James grabbed a chair from the desk and moved it up next to the bed. "The healers say he lost an eye. He'll have a permanent deformity to his face unless some kind of reconstructive surgery is done. But no brain damage, and the rest of his body should mend back properly. So he's doing pretty good for someone who should be dead."

Minni blanched, nearly spilling the water.

"It's your parents' job to hold your hand, Minni," James replied bluntly. "I'm going to straight up say it: the council doesn't care about you. All they see are direct violations of some of our core rules. And a perfect excuse to do the very thing we warned you about so many times."

"I wasn't going to let him die," was all she could manage to say, but it came out sharp.

"I know," James said softly. "But they are going to fault you for that. There is no question you killed someone, a normal human no less. His nam—"

"Don't," Minni stopped him. "I don't want to know."

James watched her for a moment, then said, "Okay."

She wiped at her eyes, trying not to cry, not now, not yet. There would be time for it later.

"Your father is arguing self-defense," he continued. "But the fact remains that the man was no longer a threat when you started draining his life. I say manslaughter but some of the councilors are hedging murder two."

"I did it to save David," Minni raised her voice, then slunk back. "I was saving a life."

"By taking another." James' words were soft, but hardly meant to be comforting. "If it were anyone else, we may be able to play those cards. But this is you, Minni. You have a unique place in the magical world. Your abilities make you a natural defense against the TechnoMages. These councilors, when they see you, they don't see a scared young woman who was just trying to save her brother… They see a weapon that's given them something to hold over it."

"So, that's it then." Minni took a deep breath. "I'm to be locked away until they have use of me?"

"That's what some of them want, yes."

Minni wiped at her noise and eyes quickly, still holding back tears. "As long as David's okay."

James frowned at his niece. "My options are limited, but I'm not going to let them lock you up indefinitely."

Three days later the council finally agreed on a course of action to take with Minni Masterson, the murdering witch who could live in both worlds. She was informed that she was not going to be put to death. Her punishment for her crime was still pending consideration.

Two days after that, it was decided Minni wouldn't be locked up either. It would cost the council far too much to keep her incarcerated in the magic-dampening cell.

The next day, Minni was told to choose what cell she wanted to live in.

"Why can't I just go home?" she asked her uncle.

"Because they want you under their thumb," he replied bluntly. "And the best way to do that is to separate you from your support mechanism."

"You are my least favorite uncle right now," Minni muttered. "Except maybe for Uncle Todd."

"You'll be allowed some visits, and there's always the senders," James continued, undeterred. "You won't be alone in this. I promise."

Minni had nothing to say, nothing substantial anyway.

James picked up a marker and wrote a large X on a map laying on the desk. "California is out, that's TechnoMage territory. Probably best not Chicago either, they have their own problems there." He crossed out the area, then moved down and drew a line through Lexington, Kentucky.

"Why not there?" Minni asked. "Isn't it a low magic zone?"

"It's a *no* magic zone," James clarified. "Absolutely no magic is to be performed inside Lexington, Kentucky, or its surrounding towns."

"Why?"

"I don't know," he admitted. "It's just been like that for the past thirty... forty years. Anyway, I didn't think you wanted to go someplace where you couldn't use your magic at all."

"Thanks." She tried to sound appreciative, all things considered. "What's left then?"

They talked for another two hours, marking off locations and putting question marks on others. Minni wanted to stay as close to Nebraska as she could, but conceded that the farther away she was from the council's grasp, the better.

The Mid-Western Council that is. There were a multitude scattered across the continent, across the world. Some strictly regional, others broken down to municipal level. And like countries, they all got along, to a point. They had their own version of a nuclear bomb and mutually assured destruction. If the world found out that magic was indeed real, then no one would be safe.

This kept conflict from ever breaking out, but it simply meant wizards had become fluent in the art of passive aggressive pettiness.

"Where is the absolutely last place the council ever wants to go?" Minni finally asked. "Any council?"

"Um..." James looked over the map. "In the US? It would be New York City, if I were to guess."

"Then I want to go there." Minni pointed to the name on the map.

"Okay." James didn't argue her choice, starting to put everything away. "I'll let the council know."

Minni was allowed to return to Purdue to finish out her last semester of school. It was only two months, and the Council knew a bridge too far when they saw one. They had what they wanted: Minni Masterson under their thumb. Might as well let her get her degree so she could support herself until they called on her. However, she was forbidden from using magic in that time.

Those last two months were three decades long and five minutes short.

Minni finished up her final classes, got her assignments done on time, passed her tests. Her college friends worried for her, said she had turned into something of a ghost. They knew most of the story of David, how he almost died, but not that she murdered a man to save his life. They tried to be there for her, and Minni smiled, Minni laughed, Minni lied, whatever she needed to do to make them stop looking at her like she was a broken doll that was probably possessed by a poltergeist.

"You never returned my texts" Her sort-of-boyfriend said, standing outside her dorm room.

"Yes," she replied.

"Is this your way of breaking up with me?"

"Pretty much."

"Do you… want to talk about this?" he asked.

"We are talking about it."

"Not… like this?"

"Look." Minni sighed, too tired to do more than a half-attempt at a shrug. "I'm leaving after I graduate. I'm going to New York. And I'm sure you've noticed, but I'm also a shitty ass girlfriend. So… I can offer you break up sex but that's about it."

Minni's graduation from Purdue was a bittersweet event. Everyone was truly proud of Minni, the first magical Masterson to get a college degree since technology invaded higher learning. With the help of some magic talismans which took a week to make, and Minni's ability to siphon off the excess, the whole family attended. Except David, of course.

The day after she officially returned from Purdue, the Councilman Ethan Galena came to the house. It was time for Minni to go. Her mother hugged Minni tight. Her father looked regretful that he hadn't done more. Her younger sister had to be restrained, left to sit in the back kitchen before she made things worse. David didn't leave his room.

Minni was allowed two large suitcases, no magic items.

"It's all just for show," her father promised her. "After a few months, they'll go lax, and you'll be able to bring more stuff from home."

Minni, the Councilman, and her Uncle James walked to the nearest Shadow Gate. It sat down the road inside what looked like a wooden bus shelter. Many wizards lived out in the country-side, all gathered around a central gate. It made things easier that way. James pulled along one case, the Councilman complained about mud on his shoes.

Making good time, they soon stood outside the Mercury Shop, in Brooklyn. Minni could feel the magic swirling around the building, a beacon in an otherwise barren landscape. Strong wards caged the building which glowed with vibrant intensity, at least in the eyes of a wizard. A wooden sign hung in the window, a the small display of leather-bound books and mason jars of teas and herbs presented a purpose of something benign.

"We're early," James pointed out as a car drove past, the exhaust an assault on their senses. "Shall we wait?"

"No." Galena pulled open the door and stepped inside.

James grabbed the door that Galena hadn't bothered to hold for them as it tried to close. He held it as Minni walked in, suitcase rolling behind her. She gave him a muddled thanks, then looked around the shop. Just as from the outside, the Mercury Shop was innocuously occultist.

A woman with long brown hair and wearing a smock dress perused the dried herbs section, picking out what she wanted and putting the tins in a small basket. She barely acknowledged them. Galena was a Councilman, not of this region, let alone district, but any magic user could look at him and know his status. The woman was a wizard and was obviously not impressed with him. Minni didn't know who she was, but liked her already.

Behind the counter, a man in his mid-thirties with baby faced skin and wannabe surfer spiked hair, flipped through a ledger. He looked up to greet them, but his words died on his lips. There was a slight frown as he glanced at the ticking clock on the wall. "You're early."

"That isn't a problem, is it?" Galena's tone was somewhere in the vicinity of not-polite.

"It's fine," the man replied, walking around the counter and heading past them, towards the door. "Hey, Arid, I'll be a bit. Just write down what you grab and I'll put it on your tab."

"I will," the woman with the herbs said. "Thank you."

The man turned the open sign around to closed and Minni could feel the sudden change in the wards throughout the building. It was an impressive little trick, she could appreciate the work. He then gestured them forward. "Let's head into the back room."

They made their way into the employee only area at the back of the shop. The whole place seemed to be designed to look normal, mundane, unless you knew what you were looking for. From the shelving full of office supplies to the owner's shirt, which said 'my patronus is that old book smell,' one might think this was just some hipster place for magical tourists. But Minni could feel the magic seeping through the very seams of the building, hiding in plain sight and on the floors above.

"You must be Dominque," the man said and she snapped her attention to him. "I hear you go by Minni. Is it okay if I call you that?"

"Yeah, sure." Minni shrugged.

"My name is Phillip McCree." He offered his hand. "You can call me Phil."

Minni switched over holding onto her luggage from her right to her left, irrationally not wanting to let go of it just yet. She took Phil's hand and gave it an easy shake.

"Mr. McCree," Galena started to say, "has agreed to be your contact in this… city. You'll come by once a week for the first six months to check in, confirm you are still abiding by the stipulations of your parole."

"After six months," Phil quickly added, "then it will be only once a month."

"Provided you have behaved yourself." Galena was not a nice person, but that had already been established.

"Do you have a place to stay?" Phil asked, ignoring the man and speaking directly to Minni.

"No," Minni admitted. "I've done some researching, but I need to do my final interview at an engineering firm to make sure I actually have a job."

"No worries." Phil smiled sympathetically and Minni kind of wanted to punch him. At least it was easy to hate Galena. "There's an apartment area upstairs. You can stay there for a couple of weeks as you settle into life here in New York."

"Thanks," Minni mumbled awkwardly.

"Are we done then?" Galena said impatiently.

"Just about," James finally spoke up, pushing Minni's second suitcase off to the side. "I would like to speak to Minni for a moment before we leave her here."

"Very well," Galena replied reluctantly and immediately walked back into the front.

Phil moved to leave, but James stopped him, asking, "Did you get the stuff I sent ahead?"

"Yes." He nodded. "I'll take care of it after you leave."

"Thank you," James replied and then waited for Phil to exit before addressing Minni again. "Six months. Just make it that long, and then the council will be too far away, and too engrossed in elections, to make you a priority."

"But I still can't go home," she reminded him.

"You'll be able to visit soon." He tried to be positive. "It will take more time for the rest, but it will come. You're not going to be stuck here forever."

"Forever is only a few days longer than a very long time," Minni retorted with a bit of a snort. "Whatever. The Copper Knight waited years. Patience is the moral of the story, right?"

"Something like that." James sighed, glancing around. "I'll be in touch, but I don't know when I'll see you again. The point is to let the council forget you are here."

"Right." Minni finally let her suitcase sit up on its bottom, pushing the handlebar down into it.

"Do you… want a hug or anything?" he asked awkwardly. "Before I go?"

"Not particularly," she replied dryly.

"Okay then." He didn't seem too terribly hurt. The Masterson side of the family was not a very affectionate bunch. "If you need anything, let me know."

"Sure."

James cleared his throat and then headed out. It was blissfully quiet in the room except for the melodic ticking of two clocks, one slightly off from the other. Something inside her howled and screamed, wanting to lash out at what was being done. But the other half accepted her fate. She had broken the rules, so what did she expect?

The shop owner, Phil, returned only a short moment later. Or maybe it was an hour. Minni had become trapped in a liminal space as she contemplated her future.

"I know it's going to be rough," Phil said as he moved over to a filing cabinet, pulling open a drawer. "I think you'll find me just but fair. I know what happened, and why you did it. You've been given a raw deal."

"Rules are rules," Minni muttered, shoving her hands in her pockets.

"Most rules, yes." Phil returned from the cabinet holding out a padded envelope. The closer it got to her, the more she felt what was inside. It was familiar and comforting, a promise of a light shining in the darkness.

Phil popped the envelope open and held it out like a bag of chips. Minni reached in without prompting, grabbing the metal within. She took the bracelet and slipped it onto her wrist. Energy coursed through her veins and tingled her skin.

"Feeling better?"

"Physically, yes," Minni sighed as she twisted and melded the copper against her skin. "In general though, that's going to take a while."

"Well, let's get your bags upstairs," he said as he moved over to the second suitcase. "Then after you get settled in, we can go get some food or something."

"I'm not really hungry," she told him as she pulled the handle back out of her suitcase.

"The point of the offer was to get you out of here for a bit," he replied with a sigh. "I don't want you to feel like you're a prisoner or something."

"Oh..." It had perhaps not crossed her mind that while she was a prisoner in this city, she might also be one in the shop.

"You know, there's a Dunkin down the road." He started rolling the suitcase towards the stairs. "We can get something light and I'll show you the area."

Minni followed him. "What's a Dunkin?"

COPLEN

THREE[3]

Tuesday, January 30th, 2018
10:08pm

"Oh, okay," Ryan said after it clicked into place about my dad's side being Irish. "Nice to meet you, Mr. Masterson."

"Ryan," he greeted politely, then turned back to me. "I take it you're bailing out Phil?"

"Yep. Just finished the paperwork." And as soon as I said the words, the other door opened. Phil walked out with Detective Longtree following behind.

Phil saw Ryan and I first, giving us a thankful smile. He saw Uncle James, not looking terribly surprised by his presence.

"Mr. Masterson," Longtree addressed my uncle with a very familiar but neutral tone. "I got nothing else to tell you."

"Oh, I know," Uncle James replied in that lawyer tone that was completely ineffable. "Phil is a friend. Representing him in this matter wouldn't constitute a conflict of interest. Am I right?"

It's troubling how many times I find myself in situations where I have no idea what is going on. But is it more worrisome that I usually prefer not knowing?

"Give it a few days and Walt will drop the charges," Longtree said he handed Phil his courier bag, complete with an evidence tag still attached to it. "The arrest was more for show than anything. He won't want to pursue this."

"No, I don't think he would." Uncle James smiled.

Longtree ignored Uncle James and kept talking to Phil. "Stay away from the Blakesleys. This happens again, I'll be less incline to be helpful, magic or no."

"Understood." Phil looked like a puppy who had his tail stepped on because he wouldn't get out from under someone's feet. It wasn't an emotion he wore well.

Uncle James held the door and we filed back out into the cold. "It's a short drive," he said, "but I can give you a lift back to the Fort if you like."

"You should take him up that offer," Phil said. "I appreciate you coming and bailing me out, but you should both go home."

Ryan and I exchanged glances.

"Okay, now we have to stay," Ryan said.

"Wanna tell us what all that was all about back there?" I asked both Phil and Uncle James.

"It's personal business," Phil answered. "I'll take care of it. You two go home, where it's warm."

I frowned. "The words you are speaking are having the opposite effect of what you're wanting."

"I don't know about you three," Uncle James interrupted, "but it's cold out here. There's a Dunkin' Donuts that's open until midnight, I believe. Why don't we sit down over a coffee and sort this out?"

I perked up at the mention of my unhealthy obsession. "Did I ever tell you that you're my favorite Uncle?"

"Considering you have six to choose from," he said dryly, very well knowing he is not my favorite uncle. "I'll take that as high praise."

"Really, just five. I mean, Uncle Todd? Is anyone going to put him at the top of their list?"

Uncle James stared blankly at me for a solid ten seconds, then turned and headed down the street. "The car is over here."

"What about Uncle Todd?" Ryan asked. "What did he do?"

"It involved dire penguins. Don't worry about it."

Despite Ryan's best efforts to get me to expand on that little piece of Masterson family history, we piled into Uncle James' rental car and drove the short distance to Dunkin's.

Yeah, so, Uncle James, despite being a Masterson descended of the First Master's sixth son, has no magic. He wasn't born with the innate ability to touch and use his aura like other wizards. Sometimes it's just like that. It has sparked a many of debates in the community about magic and genetics over the years, even before we knew about DNA. We still don't know if magic is connected to genetics. And, to be honest, the whole discussion is rife with dodgy racist undertones.

Anyway, Uncle James could have become a magician if he wanted to. Nothing was stopping him from learning how to use spells and potions that don't require the use of one's aura. But he decided he'd rather become a lawyer instead. His clients are mostly wizards, of course, which means he has no real specialty. He just goes where he's needed.

Like when one of his nieces commits murder.

"Don't judge me," Ryan said as he tore open the wrapping on the first of two sandwiches. "I haven't eaten dinner yet."

"It's nearly ten-thirty," Phil admonished.

"And you assaulted someone," he retorted, practically shoving the entire ham, egg, and cheese into his mouth.

Phil rolled his eyes and slunk into his booth seat like a petulant child and leaned against the window. Not wanting to antagonize him until he had a chance to de-sulk some, I looked at Uncle James who sat across from me, having blocked in Phil. "What brings you here?"

"Probate." Uncle James tasted his coffee, blanching slightly. He grabbed a sweetener packet. "And elder in the Blakesley family passed away two months ago without a will. I've been called in as a neutral party to help in distributing the assets."

"I thought the government got everything if someone died without a will?" I've honestly never really put a lot of thought into it. Considering how my life has been going the past few months, I should probably look into a will myself.

I mean, seriously. Since September I've been attacked by no less than four goat-grizzly-bear shadow creatures, used as a bowling ball by a gold dragon, attacked twice by pixies, nearly drowned in a pool portal, and was beaten bloody by a rich douche's henchmen. Oh, and there is a fae out there who may or may not be scheming against me. Also, I had a hella case of dysmenorrhea last month—unrelated—but I was pretty sure I was going to die then, too.

"That's not how it works, for humans at least. Like many supernatural communities, werewolves are exempt from certain laws," Uncle James explained. "It's hard to keep specific details secret in a court. So, in this case, since there isn't a will or an easy consensus between the immediate family members, a third party has been asked to make the final determinations."

"Third party being you."

"I handled a similar case last year with a family of werebears living near the Skeena River."

"Wait a sec." Ryan held his hand in front of his mouth full of food because he's polite like that. "Aren't the Blakesleys the same people Phil was told to stay away from?"

I did not catch that.

"Phil's dealings with the Blakesleys and the probate case are not related," Uncle James answered.

"Coincidence, huh?" I don't like coincidences. Not lately anyway. "Alright Phil, what is going on? You're not acting like yourself. I'd almost think you were possessed or something, but I know you better than that."

"It's personal, family business." Phil nearly huffed and grabbed his coffee from where it had been sitting, getting cold.

Ryan and I looked at each other, then back at him, staring blankly into his soul so he would get the hint. I mean, sure, Phil and I have a complicated relationship, (him being my warden and all), but he's like a second cousin to me. One that I actually like. And Ryan, well, Ryan is everyone's little brother. Mine, Phil's, and probably Uncle James' now, too. Wait, does that mean Ryan is my little brother and my uncle now?

"It's about my brother, Henry," Phil gave in and told us.

Phil only had one sibling, an older brother. Phil is actually the reverse of Uncle James. Everyone in Phil's family is normal. Phil was the only one born with magic. His parents aren't Forsakens either, which are people who have given up magic or have ancestors who did. In fact, other than a possible branch of the family dating back to the 1600s, none of the McCrees of his direct linage seem to have ever been magic users.

Like I said, sometimes it just happens like that.

"Okay, so what about Henry?" I asked, grabbing another munchkin from the sack.

"He's going to get married and settle down, announced his engagement to a local girl," Phil said like this wasn't a good thing.

"Congrats?" Ryan was just as confused as me.

"It was congrats," Phil was almost bitter, "until he said she was a werewolf and he was going to become one to be with her."

Uncle James sipped at his coffee like he'd heard all this before and was mentally creating a grocery list while he waited for things to be over. This did nothing to distill me with any confidence that this wasn't going to be a long ass night.

"Seven months," Phil kept going now that he started, his hand animatedly moving in front of his face. "Seven months he has known this woman. Seven months and he wants to settle down and become a werewolf. My brother. The man has never had a relationship that made it to the two year mark."

"It's called growth," I offered because I'm not really good at giving advice. That's normally Phil's job. "Or, you know, he's found his true love and doing right by it."

Phil tilted his head ever so slightly, giving me the blankest of expressions. "Really, Minni?"

"Just because my relationship with Marcel is basically a balancing act of chainsaws and porcelain plates on broken sticks covered in duct tape doesn't make my thoughts invalid." It got eerily quiet in the Rome Dunkin Donuts. "Too real, right?"

"We'll deal with you later." Ryan patted me on the head then turned back to Phil. "Why are you so worked up over this? If it's not going to last, then it won't, it's about them, not you."

"It matters because he wants to become a werewolf," Phil argued. I've honestly never seen him like this. "You know how bad of an idea that is?"

"So he wants to be a werewolf?" I probably said a bit too loudly, but we were the only ones in there besides the two people on staff. "When did you start telling people how to live their lives?"

Phil brought his hand up and pointedly said, "He's making an irreversible decision after only knowing this woman for seven months. Once he becomes a werewolf, there is no going back. And werewolves, they're pack animals. If he gets kicked out of the pack because they break up, there is no way to know if another pack will take him in. And you know what happens to lone wolves? They die quick, lonely, miserable deaths because they can't exist without the pack."

"You just want him to wait before joining the furry ranks?" Ryan asked. "Is that it?"

"Yes."

"Did you tell him that?"

"Yes."

"And how did that go?" I asked.

"The damn fool is still going to go through with it." Phil flopped back against the booth seat.

I've only met Phil's brother Henry maybe a handful of times. He seemed like an alright fella. The kind of person you don't mind getting stuck next to at Christmas dinner, but you wouldn't go out of your way to keep in touch with. That's how it is when you don't really have anything in common with someone.

"These Blakesleys," I wanted to clarify something. "Is this the werewolf family he wants to marry into?"

"Yeah," Phil answered.

Uncle James was more helpful. "They are part of the Lowell pack. They live just outside the city limits. They've been here since the late 1800s. The various families owned a good deal of this area: farms, dairies, copper mills, a bank."

"So, old money," I mused, then asked Phil. "Why did you get into a fight with, ah, Walt, was it?"

"The man who died was Jeremiah Blakesley, he was the grandfather of Henry's fiancé, Clara." Phil practically fumed at the thought of someone speaking of his brother like that. "Clara's father, Robert, is expected to get the lion's share of the inheritance. Walter is Jeremiah's brother and he accused Henry of being a gold-digger of low breeding."

I resisted the urge to point out that this guy was basically on Phil's side about not letting his brother turn. Of course, Walt's reasoning was hella insulting and deserved a fist to the face if you ask me. But then my typical first reaction is to punch my way through a situation. Phil's usually much more thoughtful than me.

Ugh, *family*.

They change all the rules.

"When's the wedding?" I asked, blindly digging into my sack for another munchkin.

"The spring," Phil answered. "But they want to do the turn in the morning. Something about the super blood blue moon."

I had completely forgotten about that happening. I mean, it was all over the news and stuff. I think that's why Marcel's coworker took off for the week. They traveled to get a better view of it. Astrotourism is actually big business.

I was formulating my response as I bit into a munchkin. I got two chews in and then started to spit it out.

"You okay?" Uncle James asked.

"They're still serving pumpkin flavored munchkins," I muttered as I cleared my mouth of debris, Ryan practically shoving a napkin in my face. "One slipped in."

"I thought you loved pumpkin pie?"

"Yeah, things change." I grabbed my drink, which was now closer to room temperature, and downed it to wash the taste out of my mouth.

"Okay." Ryan took the attention off me and asked Phil, "if the turning ceremony is in the morning, are you planning on doing anything to stop it?"

"I don't know." Phil shook his head. "I've tried talking to him. He won't listen."

"Are you sure stopping him is the right thing?" Ryan asked far too seriously for someone only nineteen.

Phil seemed stumped for an answer.

A cop car and unmarked cruiser pulled up outside, clearly visible through the large glass windows of the shop. Longtree stepped out and I had seen that look before on a police detective.

I cleared my throat. "I'm going to go out on a limb here and caution everyone not to make any sudden moves."

We all sat pretty still as Longtree made his way into the shop, eyes never leaving us. I had my back to him as he approached the booth, so I watched him in the reflection off the far wall. I didn't think my life was in danger, but I had a feeling the next few minutes were going to suck.

"Detective," Uncle James greeted him neutrally.

"Mr. McCree, I'm going to have to ask your whereabouts since you left the station." Longtree got right to the point.

"We came straight here." Uncle James answered for Phil, lightly gestured towards the counter. "I'm the sure barista will confirm when we arrived. There is also the matter of security footage, if it's that important."

Longtree chewed on his cheek, glancing between all of us.

Phil sat up a little straighter. "What's going on?"

"Walter Blakesley was just found dead, in his backyard," the detective answered bluntly. "He was murdered."

"Not it," I said out loud, because apparently antagonizing cops is just a thing that I do now.

FOUR[4]

**Tuesday, January 30th, 2018
10:36pm**

Everyone stared at me as I slowly pushed a half-crumbled piece of paper towards Detective Longtree. "We have receipts."

"Phil," Uncle James said calmingly as Longtree picked up the time-stamped Dunkin receipt. "I'm going to remind you it is within your rights and best interests not to say anything at this juncture."

Understatement runs in my family.

"What happened?" Phil asked, only moderately obeying instructions.

"Stabbed, with a silver dagger." Longtree was blunt.

"You're welcome to search me and my belongings," Phil replied and Uncle James gave him the side eye. I mean, obviously Phil is innocent, but volunteering to let a cop go through your stuff? Dude is off his game.

Longtree twitched, just slightly. It was hard to tell what it meant in context. All he said was, "Don't leave Rome. I have eyes on Stanwix, and checkpoints on the roads."

"Noted." Uncle James nodded and I think he might have kicked Phil under the table.

After another cursory glance, Longtree headed out to his car. He said something to the uniform standing outside. Both men got back into their vehicles, but only Longtree left. The other guy continued to sit there, watching us, because, well yeah.

"This doesn't make any sense," Uncle James said what we were all thinking. "Walter Blakesley wasn't in line to receive much of the share from his cousin's holdings. In fact, he wasn't even part of the debate."

"Why?" Ryan asked the sensible question.

"Despite his many short comings, he's not--he wasn't--a greedy man." Uncle James pulled his phone out of his pocket and started to mess around on it. "He already had a large share of his own wealth. All he wanted was *Le Bosquet d'Argus*. No one argued the claim. It's the profitable land and business shares that no one can agree on."

"Maybe it was a crime of passion?" Ryan suggested. "It's not related to anything else that's happened?"

"After the last six months we've had?" I snorted.

Ryan's brows shot up. "Oh, you think Drake will show up again and bring more chocolate?"

"God, you've been spoiled." I didn't really mean it, but Ryan didn't argue with me either, so...

"It's getting late," Uncle James said as he checked his watch. "Phil, where are you staying?"

"I... hadn't thought that far ahead when I got here this morning," he admitted, thoroughly lost. Seriously, I have never seen him so disorganized and not... well, Phil. He was acting far too much like me, and frankly, I'm enough to handle. "I really need to call my brother."

"I rented a house since I wasn't sure how long I'd be here," Uncle James said. "Why don't we head over there? You can call Henry. Hopefully Detective Longtree will make an arrest tonight and you can go back to New York."

We grabbed—okay, I grabbed—the last of the munchkins and we headed to Uncle James' car. Ryan waved at the policeman before hopping in. How the kid has never been arrested, I will never know. Me on the other hand... I've lost count.

Uncle James drove while I enjoyed the scenery of the town. Dark, quiet, dusting of snow... yeah, it was pretty.

The rental house was a nice little Craftsman that was probably as old as the town. It was tucked in with a bunch of other houses lining a road that wasn't designed with cars in mind. A pre-fab car cover sat next to the house, squeezed up against the neighbor's fence. It looked really out of place with the timber and brick of the classic Craftsman.

A car was out front, blocking one lane, and four men were sitting on the porch.

"You know these guys?" Phil asked as we pulled up under the car cover.

I started diverting magic into my bracelet, just in case.

"They're Blakesleys," Uncle James said, putting the car in park and killing the engine.

We piled out and I saw the police car park farther down the road where there was space. I wasn't terribly surprised that they had followed us.

"Gentlemen," Uncle James said, stepping onto the porch.

"Have you heard about Walter?" asked the leader, a tall looking gent in his thirties whose muscles probably had muscles. I was sure I could hear Ryan drooling behind me.

"We've been informed."

"You." The leader pointed at Phil. "You are the one who punched him earlier today."

"And that's all I did," Phil defended himself as a murmur ran through the group.

"Gerald," Uncle James said tiredly. "I would like to remind you that Phil was in police custody for most of the night. Then he was with me, in a public location. He couldn't have committed the murder."

"Maybe not himself." Gerald looked at me and Ryan. "But what about one of his pack?"

"We're not a pack," I said, then totally second guessed myself. "Wait, are we?"

"We're a coven," Ryan answered thoughtfully. "And that's kinda like a pack, right?"

"I suppose it's how you define pack."

"Minni." Uncle James added a non-verbal 'shut up.'

Gerald stepped forward and sniffed the air slightly. "You understand, sir, if we don't simply take your word for it."

"There's a reason why it's inadmissible in court." Uncle James was really starting to take on the lawyer voice. "And it would be a violation without consent."

"I consent," Phil said.

"Phil!" Uncle James added a *very* non-verbal 'shut the hell up' to his name.

"I didn't kill Walter Blakesley and I need to talk to Henry," Phil was uncharacteristically all over the place. "Once I can show the former, then I can do the latter."

Ryan whispered, "You know what he's talking about?"

"They're speaking English but that's all I got," I admitted.

Phil had already pulled his coat sleeve up and held his arm out towards Gerald. The man stepped forward, took Phil's arm, and proceeded to literally sniff his wrist. I was completely stunned into silence. Doesn't happen often. Gerald let go of Phil and gave a satisfying nod of his head.

"Alright, Mr. McCree," Gerald said. "I believe you did not personally murder Uncle Walt."

"What just happened?" I asked dumbly.

"The lycanthrope version of a lie detector test." Uncle James gave a heavy sigh. "And it is about as reliable as an actual lie detector, which is to say, not reliable at all."

Gerald got testy at that. "You rather I continued believing this man murdered my uncle?"

"I'd rather you relied on the actual evidence," Uncle James replied drolly.

"Doesn't mean one of his pack didn't do it."

Okay, so this was a rather lame episode of *CSI: NY, Rome Edition*. I was kind of with Phil on that. I just wanted to move on with my life and let the cops sort out the murder mystery. I turned to Uncle James. "Is there a downside to him sniffing us?"

"He'll have your complete scent," he answered.

"And that's bad why?"

Uncle James sighed. "It can tell things about you, can be used to hunt you down. But mostly, it's the principle of the thing. It's your scent, as unique to you as your blood."

"Well," Ryan said after a moment of consideration, "if Phil is okay with giving his, then I'm okay, too. Let's just get it over with so I can go inside where it's warm."

Ryan lifted his hand and pulled back his sleeve. Uncle James just shook his head, scratching at his brow. You know, if he wanted to be a lawyer so bad, maybe he shouldn't keep wizards as clients.

We are the *worst*.

Gerald took Ryan's arm and did the same sniff against his wrist. After a good five second count, he tilted his head and looked up at Ryan.

"What?" Ryan asked.

"Nothing of importance." Gerald let him go. "You did not kill Uncle Walt."

Duh. Anyone who's known Ryan for longer than five minutes could have told him that. Ryan couldn't kill anyone. Now, would he sell my left kidney for backstage passes to his favorite band and a lifetime supply of thermal underwear?

Eh, probably.

With a shrug of my shoulders, I pulled up the right arm sleeve of my coat and offered my own wrist to be sniffed. I've honestly had way worse propositions when going out clubbing with Stacey. At least this guy asked permission first before taking my arm and getting a sniff.

"You smell of copper," Gerald said as he let go, his face slightly confused.

I pulled back the sleeve of my left arm to show my copper focus bracelet. "I get that a lot."

He looked confused for a second, then shook it off. His attention was now on Uncle James who was entirely done with all of us. But with a slightly over dramatic sigh, he gave in and let Gerald sniff him as well. This led to a nice little double take as Gerald looked between me and Uncle James.

"You two are related," Gerald said, somewhat confused.

Uncle James fixed his sleeve. "Are you satisfied?"

"Yes, thank you." Gerald seemed to be pretty honest with us. He trusted his nose over the evidence, but hey, as long as he wasn't barking up the wrong tree.

Ah, sorry, no pun intended. Honest.

"We'll leave you now," Gerald said, gesturing to the other three. "We will find out who did this."

As ominous statements go, I rated it about a seven.

Gerald and his group walked down to the vehicle and left. The policeman in his car just sat there and continued to watch us. I wasn't terribly surprised by that.

"Can I borrow your phone?" Phil asked as we headed into the house.

"Sure." I handed it over after making sure there weren't any notifications that needed to be dealt with. Phil pulled a piece of paper out of his pocket and started to dial.

The house my uncle rented was pretty sparse, as one would expect from a one-size-fits-all rental. The furniture was nice, but bland enough not to offend and cheap enough not to be missed should it be broken. A shit ton of paperwork lay spiraled across the kitchen table. There did seem to be a pattern in the chaos though.

"Is this the probate case?" I asked Uncle James.

"Hey, Clara," Phil said into the phone as he wandered off into, well, I'm not sure even he knew where he was going. "It's Phil. Can you give the phone to Henry?"

Uncle James took off his coat and put it on the back of a chair. "Yes. Still sorting out everyone's claims."

"So, Walter Blakesley and this dead guy Jason—"

"Jeremiah."

"Right. Phil said he and Walter were brothers?"

"Yes." Uncle James picked up a family tree from the pile. "Gerald is the grandson of a third brother, which makes Walter his grand-uncle as well. Walter had no children of his own."

"Gerald was rather upset Did Walter take a special interest in him or something?" I asked, picking up more papers.

"No more than the others, but with the probate case he did take Gerald's side on some claims."

I barely had a chance to really look at anything when Phil yelled from somewhere in the house. "What do you mean Henry was arrested for murder?!"

Yeah… probably should have seen that coming.

37

Yeah… probably should have seen that coming.

FIVE[5]

June 8th, 2013

Minni wasn't sure why she was surprised that finding a decent apartment in New York City was turning into some kind of survival game show. She'd find a listing but the apartment would be gone before she could look into it. Or one of her potential roommates kept calling her Dominican, even after she clearly stated she was Cheyenne.

She wondered if screaming in frustration would even be noticed on a NYC bus.

"Just checking in," Uncle James texted. *"No troubles?"*

*"I am going out of my mind and I'm *this* close to leveling this city with an EMP,"* she wrote out, then after a long, deep sigh, she deleted it and instead sent. *"So far, so good."*

"Glad to hear."

Minni hopped off at the next stop. It was an alternate route service bus because the subway line she had been taking was down for some reason or another. But she was pretty sure she got onto the wrong bus. She hadn't quite gotten used to relying on public transportation, but if she was honest, she wasn't really paying attention to the signs.

Knowing that Phil would send out a search party if she didn't return at a decent time, Minni put all her brain power towards understanding which bus and/or subway she was supposed to get on. She had no one but herself to blame when she realized she had to walk three or so blocks to get to a different stop because she had indeed gotten on the wrong bus.

She set off down a side street lined with a smattering of single family homes and apartment buildings all squashed together. Cars lined either side with trees barely managing to find a space between them and the walkway.

Minni stopped when she noticed a sign stuck on a little fence guarding the windows of the bottom floor. In inhumanly neat writing with a bold marker it said there was a room for rent, third floor, inquire within, buzzer 3B. She stared at it, rereading it several times as if there was a code she was missing.

The area looked decently nice. It was close to the bus stop that she needed. And it was on the third floor.

"Can't be that easy," Minni sighed continue walking.

She halted after three steps and turned back. Nothing ventured, nothing gained, and it would annoy her for days that she didn't at least check.

"Hello?" a woman answered when Minni hit the buzzer.

"Hi, uh, my name Dominque Masterson," she replied as she looked up at the camera. "I saw your sign about the room. Is it still available?"

"I put that out like half an hour ago." The woman was trying to sound surprised but everything in her voice failed her. The door clicked. "Come on up."

Minni took the elevator to the third floor, knocking lightly on the appropriate apartment. A blonde woman a few years older than her opened the door. Her clothing was BoHo-Chic, or at least that's how it would be explained to Minni later. It felt like the woman tried too hard to look like a farm hand, without the hard work. Minni was suitably not impressed.

The woman gave Minni a once-over. Likely trying to decide if it was worth her effort to let her in. Or if it would be a really bad idea in general to have anything to do with Minni.

"Dominque, you said?" The woman offered her hand. "I'm Gillian, you can call me Gilly."

"Nice to meet you, Gilly," Minni smiled as best she could as they shook hands. "And you can call me Minni."

"Minni, great." Gilly smiled and moved aside so she could enter the apartment which... was not what Minni expected.

She walked right into the main sitting area, very neutral with a sofa, chairs, and a tv up on the wall between two doors. A kitchen lined the back wall, pretty standard except for the industrial fridge which seemed to have some kind of chores list taking up most of the door. A heavy dining table seemed to sub for a kitchen island as well. The same gray fake-stone linoleum was laid across the entire length. All in all, it was smaller than her living room back home.

"We call this the commons," Gilly said as she closed the door. "Everything is shared out here. You have your fourth of the fridge, your own cabinet, etc. Though you're welcome to have your own tv or mini-fridge in your room. You'd be responsible for your space and cleaning up after yourself."

"I'm getting college dorm vibes," Minni mumbled, though she didn't mean it disparagingly.

"Not a local, are you?" Gilly stated more than questioned, then opened one of the doors. "This would be your room."

It was a square that was big enough for maybe a twin bed, a desk, and one other piece of furniture, provided it wasn't too big. Her room growing up was bigger than this. Well, after her older sister moved out and she didn't have to share any more.

Minni nodded approvingly. It was all she really needed for the time being. She still only had the two suitcases of stuff she brought from home. And it wasn't like she did anything else but go to work, come back, eat, sleep, watch some tv or read a book. Phil had tried to encourage Minni to explore the city. There were lots of places she could go that wizards couldn't, and she idly wondered if he simply wanted to use her to be able to sightsee.

Useful. That was the term that defined Minni's life.

She was useful.

It was the only reason she was still alive.

"And here's the bathroom." Gilly ushered Minni to the door situated between the two bedrooms. The bathroom was very cramped, about enough space to be able to turn around in, and that's it. Minni knew it wasn't as wide as a tub because there was only a shower that took up the end. At least the sink had a counter with two sides, one which already looked to be claimed.

Having grown up with six siblings, Minni felt like she would have more space than she was used to.

"You would be sharing with Chelsea." Gilly gestured to the incidentals sitting on the right side of the sink.

"Chelsea?" Minni asked.

"Let me get her." Gilly smiled and started to move away. "If she doesn't like you, then I'm afraid this is a non-starter."

Made sense to Minni. They would likely find themselves awash with candidates, so might as well pick someone that didn't piss them off on sight.

Minni exited the bathroom in time to see the door to the other bedroom open after Gilly knocked on it. A woman walked out and Minni could only describe her as the quirky but trendy personal assistant type. But she smiled easily and didn't give off any bad vibes, magical or otherwise.

"Chelsea," Gilly made introductions, "this is Minni, she's our first applicant for the room."

"You put that notice out like half an hour ago," Chelsea said like she wasn't sure why she was surprised. Then she shook her head and held out her hand. "Hi, I'm Chelsea."

"Nice to meet you," Minni said as politely as she could, which meant her mid-western started to show.

Chelsea eyed her warily. "You're from Nebraska, right?"

"Uh, yeah." Minni was a little thrown at that.

"I may have lost most of my accent," Chelsea explained, "but I'm from South Dakota myself."

"Huh," Minni couldn't stop herself, deadpanning. "I won't hold it against you."

Chelsea looked blankly at her for a moment, then laughed. "Dry humor, I like it."

"Ah, well, that's a good start," Gilly said happily. "Now, I kinda made the assumption that you have a stable job."

"Oh, yeah, I just started at an engineering firm," Minni replied, pulling out her phone. "Payroll is all online. I can show you my details right now."

"It would be good to know that you can pay the rent, yes."

"Speaking of?" Minni asked as she signed into the app. "How much is rent, and how would that work?"

"Yes, well—"

Gilly was cut off as someone came quickly through the front door, a regular tornado of color and energy. She was tall with a mass of curly dark hair over her darker skin. The woman barely seemed to register them as she went straight for one of the other two bedrooms. She quickly grabbed a bag and then headed back to front door.

"Stacey!" Gilly called out to her and the woman skidded to a stop. "We're interviewing an applicant for the fourth room. Do you want some input on this?"

Stacey looked between all three of them, but it was clear she was on a mission. "Sorry, I have a literal fashion emergency. Um, what's your name?"

"Minni," she supplied.

"Are you a serial killer?"

"No." Minni blinked. "Not a *serial* killer."

"Hah! I like her, we can keep her." And with that, Stacey was out the door.

The other two laughed about Minni's serial killer 'joke,' but she had only been telling the truth. She was killer—singular victim. She had been convicted and was serving out her sentence. The two women standing before her didn't know they were living in low-magic zone that could easily be made into an open-air prison. They didn't need to know that, either.

Minni showed them that she could afford the rent and still be able to eat. That was all that mattered in the end.

But as that discussion took place, another person called about the room. Minni gave Gilly her number, not blaming them for wanting to see who else might be in need of a new apartment. As she left, Gilly gave her a promising smile that Minni took at face value of her just being polite. At this point Minni was beyond being hopeful of anything turning out in her favor. But at least she wouldn't be plagued by the what-if that would come with not having at least checked the place out.

Minni made it to the proper bus this time and found her connection to get back to the Mercury Shop. Phil was behind the counter working on inventory. He looked up when she entered, giving Minni a small sense of déjà vu.

"You're later than normal." His words weren't reproach, more like supportive, and this grated on Minni because she really wanted to hate it.

"Missed my connections," she admitted as she set her bag down on the counter. "But I happened on a room for rent, near a good bus stop. Affordable but didn't read as sketchy."

"That's good to hear," he said as he put his ledger away. "You think you'll get it?"

"Anyone's guess." Minni shrugged and pinched the bridge of her nose. "I'm this close to calling the search quits and just paying you to live upstairs."

"It's an option, but…" He trailed off with a sigh. They had already had this discussion.

Yes, New York City was an open-air prison. But Phil didn't want her to think that she was in a literal prison. Getting out into her own place would give Minni some sense of control over herself. At least that was Phil's working theory. Minni was a bit skeptical.

A prison is still a prison, no matter what shape it takes and what it has to offer.

"Who knows?" Minni sighed as she smiled. "By this time next week I should be out of your hair. Except, you know, for my weekly parole visits."

"You really shouldn't think of it like that."

"But that's exactly what they are."

Phil sighed, straightening up one of the displays. "Life throws a lot of crap at us, and sometimes it is actual crap. But if we don't make the best of it, then what's the point?"

"I'm only alive because I'm a weapon," she said bluntly. "That's the literal point."

"You shouldn't—"

"Think of it like that?" Minni said mock-cheerfully.

Phil knew a losing battle when he saw one and so he said nothing. Minni grabbed her bag and headed up the stairs to the room. She collapsed onto the bed and curled into herself. If she could have kept herself from crying, she would have.

POP!

The electrical box blew a fuse, the whole building plunged into darkness.

"Fuck."

Minni dragged herself out of bed. She used her phone to light her way back down to the bottom floor. It looked like Phil had already left to go to his own apartment and she had no idea where the breaker box was. At least there weren't any computers or security systems to worry about. The two clocks in the break room ran on batteries and she apparently didn't drain them. Just the power grid.

Not wanting to mess up anything, she figured she'd fix it in the morning and went to return upstairs. The back door jingled as someone unlocked it. Phil walked in, carryout bags in hand. He jiggled the light switch twice, not terribly surprised. It wasn't like losing power was anything new to wizards. He uttered a few short words in Latin, and all the candles in the room ignited.

"Sorry," Minni mumbled.

"You caused the outage?" Phil frowned, curious.

"It was an accident," she assured him, starting to feel small. "I probably should have mentioned, sometimes when I get upset, I draw in energy. I don't know why I do it. I just... do..."

"Oh." He sat the bags on the table. "I brought you dinner."

"... Huh?"

"Thought you could use some cheering up." Phil pulled several styrofoam containers out of the first bag. "You said you really liked that Vietnamese place down the road. I just hope you're up for spicy right now."

"Um, thanks," she mumbled, moving forward and feeling strangely lifted by the smells. "You didn't have to do this."

"You're my responsibility, Minni." He slid one of the containers across the table, closer to her. "I'm not going to sit back while you depression spiral."

"I'm not—"

Phil gave her a 'bitch, please' look and that shut her up.

Clearing her throat, Minni pulled a stool over to the table and sat down. He handed her a bottle of soda and they started in on the food. Other than the occasional request to pass something, they ate in silence. Except for two stupid clocks ticking out of time from each other.

SIX[6]

August 17th, 2013

Saturday mornings had turned into something of a routine once Minni settled into her new apartment. First, she would take a late morning walk. Then she'd stop by the Dunkin Donuts and grab herself a coffee because it was chilly weather. If there were no delays, she'd arrive at the Mercury Shop just in time for it to open. Today, she got there five minutes past nine.

The shop was still dark.

Minni could walk around to the back. She still had a key to the backdoor, but not the front. Instead, she pressed her face up to the glass and tried to see inside. Nothing looked off. Nothing felt off. But she hadn't known Phil to ever be late in opening the shop. Realizing that she only had three months of experience to gauge from, Minni wasn't too terribly worried. Just a tad bit worried.

Phil came bursting through the back, throwing his satchel around his neck while talking to two others animatedly. There was a woman, her mass of curly brown hair tied back. With her was an older man who had the same eyes and probably the same chin, but it was hard to tell with the scruff of grey beard he was sporting. Minni was pretty sure they were related, if she had to guess.

It wasn't until Phil was at the front door, unlocking it, that he noticed Minni standing out on the sidewalk. He looked straight at her and she could see the gears ticking over.

"I need you to come with us," Phil said as soon as he was outside, locking up.

"With you where?" Minni asked as she followed them.

"There's a Camazotz loose at a power plant in Astoria," Phil explained, speed walking down the sidewalk. "We were going to risk a cab, but we could use you to act as a magic sink."

"Yeah, sure." Minni had no problem keeping up with them, and she was pretty sure this wouldn't be a violation of her parole, but… "Um, what's a camazotz?"

"A death bat," the woman called over her shoulder.

"A what now?"

"It's pretty much how it sounds."

Minni questioned why she was still following them.

Phil was half off the sidewalk, trying to wave down a cab, when he decided to make introductions. "Minni, this is Eli Lange and his granddaughter, Vivian."

"Nice to meet you," Minni said politely.

"Their specialty is fire magic," Phil added.

"Oh, that's cool."

"Minni is an energy conduit," he told them. "She'll be able to keep our magic from destroying the electronics in the plant."

Minni pursed her lips. "Why, yes, Phil, I'll help you fight a *death* bat in a power plant, thanks ever so much for asking."

Someone walking past paused slightly then kept on going.

"You did order her to follow us," Vivian pointed out.

Phil looked like he was trying to come up with a way to argue her point, and utterly failed. "Sorry, we're in a hurry. There's no Shadow Gates near the plant and this could affect thousands of lives."

"And you'd just assume I'd help?" Minni asked him.

"Well, yes…"

A cab stopped and Minni sighed. "Alright, fine, let's go."

The trip from Brooklyn up through Queens took about half an hour, which was half an hour too long if you asked Phil. Minni knows, because she asked. But any other way to the Ditmars neighborhood of Astoria would have taken even longer. Minni kept checking her phone for news reports of some kind of explosion or blackout, but so far, so good.

When they got to the plant, a rather nervous looking gent was there to meet them. He wore a white and blue checked dress shirt that still had the creases in it from being folded up in whatever department store he had bought it at.

"You Phil McCree?" the man asked.

"Yes," Phil said after throwing some twenties at the cabby. "Are you Carl?"

"That's my boss," he replied. "I'll take you to him. I'm Henry, by the way."

"Henry? That'll be easy to remember." Phil nodded, Minni not yet knowing that Phil had a brother named Henry. "This is Eli, Viv, and Minni."

"I really hope you can take care of this." Henry said as he led them past the security gate.

"It will be my first Camazotz," Phil admitted. "They're native to Mexico and Central America. I don't think one has ever been sighted this far north."

"I don't care where it's from, it just needs to go."

Minni trailed silently behind the group as they were led through building after building of the massive power plant complex. If she had to guess, it had been built on over the years in various stages. The whole thing took up a block, or three. Minni wasn't sure she could get an adequate understanding of its size.

"Where is everyone?" Phil asked when they realized the area was seemingly devoid of people.

"We shut down everything except essential operations," Henry explained. "And it's a Saturday, so office staff is light."

"Smart," Minni murmured as they approached a large brick building with thin white smoke stacks. "I'm sure cornering a bat the size of a toddler in one of the turbine rooms is probably an OHSA violation."

Phil gave her a disapproving brow, but Henry looked straight at Minni with the most earnest of expressions. "Do you think so?"

Minni shrugged. "Everything is an OHSA violation."

"Phil McCree?" someone called out from the open door to the building.

"That's me," Phil answered as he walked towards the man who looked far more official with his jacket and tie, two cell phones and a Walkie clipped to his belt. "You Carl?"

"Plant Supervisor," he said as they shook hands. "Wife's a third generation Forsaken. She called around and was pointed to you. You ever dealt with one of these things?"

"No, but I've handled similar," Phil assured him.

"Good, come with me." Carl lead them inside down a short hall, and then stopped at a door. "The bat is in there, but we don't know where. It can't seem to be able to open doors or windows, so I'm not sure how it got in there in the first place."

"Really?" Phil curiously frowned. "There are no natural shadow gates around here, either."

"Details." Carl didn't seem interested in the why. "Just get rid of it. Kill it if you have to."

That snapped Phil out of his contemplations. "It shouldn't come to that."

"Whatever, just…" Carl gestured towards the door.

"Okay." Phil turned to Minni and the others. "They have extremely tough skin, so mild fireballs won't hurt it that much. Let's try to stun it so I can cast a sleep spell on it."

Minni raised her hand. "Don't you have to be basically touching the subject to cast a sleep spell on it?"

"Yes."

"Oh, okay." Minni nodded. "Luck with that."

Phil dug into his satchel to grab his blasting rod. "Minni, I need you to make sure we don't fry any of the systems in there."

"That I can do." She twisted her copper bracelet, absorbing what static was already lingering around the wizards. It would grow exponentially once they started using magic.

After sketching out a rough battle plan, Phil reached for the handle and slowly opened the door. Blasting rod slightly extended in front of him, he carefully walked into the turbine room. Vivian followed, her own blasting rod at the ready, Eli behind them.

Minni realized she could probably just stay in the hall and sink their magic from there. But she thought of this only after she had walked into the room. She figured it would be bad form to walk out again.

The turbine room was a two story tall wide open expanse. Large, nearly twelve feet tall enclosed turbines took up most of the space. Piping of all sorts snaked its way between them leading to large pumps and electrical boxes. Minni got curious, trying to determine the system flow and output based on what she could make of the visible controls on the boxes. Then she remembered there was a death bat on the loose and that was probably more important.

"Anyone see it?" Phil had went left, Vivian center, and Eli had gone to the right. The room hummed, some of the machinery still going. Carl wasn't going to shut everything down unless absolutely necessary.

"Not seeing it," Vivian called back after they walked to the various edges of the open section of the room.

"Too many places for it to hide," Eli grumbled, gesturing to the nooks between the turbines and the crannies created by the piping. Some of the pipes Minni could probably fit inside.

"Let's regroup." Phil started to walk backwards, towards the door. "We sweep the building from one side. Check every possible hiding place."

The three of them started to converge on where Minni was standing, their eyes still scanning the room. Minni blew out a breath like she was waiting on a bus that wasn't due to show for another five minutes.

"There!" Vivian shouted.

Minni turned her head in time to see something big and dark fly straight at her. She threw her arm up and reflexively created a kinetic shield using her bracelet as a focus. The death bat slammed into the kinetic barrier as if it was hitting an actual shield Minni was holding.

Absorbing kinetic energy didn't come as natural to Minni as absorbing electrical. It wasn't something she did on instinct. When the death bat hit, it hit hard, pushing against the shield even as it bounced off. Minni went flying backwards from the force of the impact. She fell and slid across the buffed concrete floor right into one of the large electrical boxes.

"Minni?" Phil called out. It sounded less like worry and more him simply confirming she was still conscious.

"I'm fine," Minni grumbled, loudly, as she got herself back into standing position. She had managed not to hit her head or anything else vital. She'd have a bruise on her thigh where she impacted against the box.

"Where did it go?" Eli asked.

None of them were going to fire unless they had a clear shot. Last thing they needed to do was cause an explosion inside of a power plant. They gathered back together, Phil scanning over Minni to make sure she was indeed okay. Once he was satisfied, he said, "We can try to lure it out."

"With what?" Vivian nearly laughed. "It's a carrion eater."

Minni ran her hand over her face. "Did you even have a plan when you walked in here?"

"Well—"

The death bat swooped down, dive bombing them in a surprise attack. Minni raised her focus again so she could project the shield, but this time she was a bit too slow on the draw. The creature grabbed her outreached arm in its clawed feet and launched itself up into the air, taking her with it.

"Minni!" Phil shouted from below.

"WHAT!?" Minni shouted back, a bit more focused on not getting her arm wrenched from her shoulder. She grabbed the leg of the death bat with her other hand, trying to take her weight off her immobilized arm. The tiny but sharp barbed ridges on the underside of the creature's talons dug into her skin through the sleeve of her cotton jacket.

The death bat was agile, carrying her weight with ease. It flew down the length of the room, Minni nearly banging her legs against some pipes that jutted over one of the turbines. Blood was starting to soak into her sleeve.

"Fuck. This. Shit."

Minni took a deep breath and electrocuted the death bat.

The creature seized up as electricity ran through it. Every muscle constricted, including its talons that bit in deeper. But when its wings closed in, they both proceeded to fall like stones from nearly two stories up.

Minni hadn't thought that part through.

With the death bat's death grip on her, there was no way she could try to tuck and roll. In the second it took her to fall one of the two stories, she decided she'd settle for a broken leg over a broken neck any day.

About seven feet from the ground, the air got thick, like molasses. At every foot, it got denser, enveloping her until she was sure she'd suffocate before hitting concrete. When her feet did touch down, it was with little more force than stepping down two steps at a time. The air returned to normal and both Minni and the death bat collapsed onto the floor with a soft thud.

The others were there in an instant, Phil immediately checking the on death bat. "You didn't kill it?"

"Voltage to amperage. It's a very important ratio," Minni mumbled, trying to pry the talons from her arm. Vivian helped her and Eli wrapped the appendage in a clean shop towel he had sourced from Phil's bag.

Phil casted a sleep spell over the death bat, making sure it wouldn't be giving them any more trouble. It started to breath slowly and peacefully, a contrast to the rest of them still trying to catch theirs from the excitement. Phil looked at her like he wanted to say something but wasn't sure.

"Where did all this blood come from?" Carl asked as he walked up with Henry.

"Oh, hi!" Minni waved ever so slightly with her bloody towel wrapped arm.

Carl grabbed his radio. "I need a first responder in the turbine room."

"On my way," someone replied.

A few minutes later, a plant worker who had taken some extra training session in first response was patching up Minni. They sat on the other side of the room, conventionally out of line of site of the sleeping death bat. Thankfully nothing needed stitches as the wounds were more punctures rather than rips.

She'd have scars for a few years, tiny specks of lightly colored skin dotted around in a neat little pattern.

"Were you bit?" the man asked.

"No, just scratched."

"Okay, then you probably didn't contract any disease," he said casually.

Minni frowned at him. "What kind of diseases?"

"I dunno," the man admitted, securing the last bandage wrap. "But if that was a wild animal, who knows what it could've been carrying."

"Thank you for telling me that." Minni was not thankful.

"You'll want to go straight to the emergency room if you start to feel sick or itchy or just anything out of place," the man said before he left, Henry showing him out.

Minni made her way back to where Phil and Vivian were wrapping the death bat up in a tarp, curtesy of Carl. The plan, from what Minni heard upon her approach, was that they were going to load it up into the back of one of the work trucks. Then they were going to drive it to the Bronx where a Shadow Gate existed that could get them to Tulum, Mexico. Phil had already contacted a local coven to meet them at the gate.

"I'm not going to turn into a death bat, am I?"

Phil gave her a startled blink. "What?"

Minni raised her bandaged arm. "A magical creature drew blood. I wanna know if I'm going to turn into one or gain bat powers or something. You know, so I can plan out my day."

"You're fine, Minni," Phil assured her and finished tying off the tarp.

"Camazotz's are not were-creatures." Vivian patted her on the shoulder. "And they aren't radioactive, either. They're just really big bats who like to snatch people's heads off."

Minni blinked. "You could have told me that earlier."

"You would have jumped out of the taxi."

"That's fair," Minni agreed. This is what she gets for googling something and only reading the search results and not the actual articles themselves.

After the Camazotz was secured, they spent a good fifteen minutes dragging the unconscious creature to a large bay door. Then another ten just getting it into the back of the truck. After a short discussion, they decided that Vivian and Eli would set in the cab with Carl while Phil and Minni sat in the truck bed with the creature. If the sleep spell started to wear off, Phil could reapply it or Minni could zap it again.

Carl didn't drive terribly fast, but the wind rushing by was enough to turn chilly into cold. Minni started to build a thermal buffer around herself.

"You cold?" she asked Phil.

"A bit." His chattering teeth gave him away.

"Here." Minni reached across the head of the Camazotz and took Phil's wrist. She sent a wave of thermal energy through his clothing. "That should at least keep your core warm."

"Thanks," he replied, appreciative.

They sat in silence for a few minutes before Minni said, "Oh, hey, I don't think I thanked you for catching me when I fell."

"No problem." He shrugged. "I figured something like that might happen—what with dealing with a flying creature, so I had the spell prepared."

"Oh, smart."

"I had a plan going in," Phil answered her question from earlier. "Not my first rodeo."

Minni tilted her head. "Have you ever been to a rodeo?"

"No," Phil faltered. "But you get the point."

"I'll have to take you to a rodeo sometime," Minni said, grinning at the idea.

"Yeah, please don't," he deadpanned.

Minni laughed until a sobering thought came to her. "Oh, hell. I electrocuted this big guy. I'm not going to get in trouble with the council, am I?"

Phil was thoughtful for a moment as the truck stopped at a red light. "You were defending yourself against an attack. I put you in that position by asking you to come with me. If there is any blow back, then it will be on me."

"I'm sorry." Minni got a horrible sinking in her stomach at that. "I don't want you to get in trouble because of me."

"Don't worry about it," he assured her. "The councils want nothing to do with this city. If I leave for any reason, it becomes their responsibility. That allows me some leeway."

"Oh," Minni said so quietly he might not have heard over the traffic.

"Look, I won't let the council violate your parole because of this," Phil said with enough confidence that Minni was inclined to believe him.

"Thanks." She tried to smile but there was still that aura of fear inside her that once again she offered the council the perfect opportunity to put her even farther under their thumb.

"You're a part of our coven, Minni," Phil continued. "To our kind, a coven is just as important as family. And we'd both do anything for our families."

SEVEN[7]

Tuesday, January 30th, 2018
11:21pm

Phil came back into the room after he finished his phone call, looking frazzled. "My brother's been arrested for the murder of Walter Blakesley."

"Yeah, we heard," I said drolly.

Uncle James started gathering up his things. "I'll get down to the station. A murder is a lot more involved than an assault. Even if I can't take Henry's case, I can at least advise him right now before he says or does something stupid."

"I'm coming with." Phil started to move to the door.

"No." Uncle James was firm as he fixed his coat. "Longtree won't let you see him. There's nothing you can do right now, and your presence will only be a distraction. Trust me, Phil. I'll take care of Henry."

For a hot second I thought Phil would argue with him and do something stupid. But he managed to tuck brother-Phil away and let coven-leader-Phil make the rational decision. "Okay, just keep me updated."

"I'll text Minni." With that assurance, Uncle James was out the door. A minute later, car headlights swung across the house and we were left there.

"So… now what?" Ryan asked.

"Good question." I sat in one of the dining table chairs because I was… well, tired of standing, to be honest. I'd been going to bed way early for the past several days so my body was a bit confused as to what mode it was supposed to be in. I didn't want to rely too much on my magic to keep me going. "Let's just wait and see what is happening with Henry."

"He's not a murderer," Phil spoke with absolute surety.

"Probably." I had real trouble with completely writing off the possibility that Henry McCree committed a murder. After all, the same was thought of me at one point. That I could never do such a thing. "Let's wait and see what the evidence says. Let the cops do their job."

Pretty sure Phil gave me a look I've given him on several occasions. "Can I keep borrowing your phone?"

"Sure." I saw no point in stopping him. "Just let me know if I get any texts."

Phil nodded and wandered off down the hall again. Ryan decided to raid the kitchen. The cupboards were bare seeing as it was a rental house. All that was there were some snack foods and basic condiments. Ryan did find lots of yogurt in the fridge, one of which he snagged.

"Do you think he'll mind?" Ryan asked, finding a spoon in the dishwasher.

"I don't think so." It was an honest enough answer. I mean, I didn't even know Uncle James liked yogurt that much. It's not like we hung out or anything. In fact, I hadn't seen him in years. Had a few calls, texts, and emails, but that was it. It wasn't like he didn't care, He was trying not to draw attention to me.

I picked up a family genealogy paper from the kitchen table and read over it. It said the Lowell Pack had been in Rome since 1817. The pack, then lead by Mary Lowell, came to Rome as laborers to help start digging the Erie Canal. I was today-years-old when I learned the canal, which stretches from Lake Erie to the Hudson River at Albany, began its construction in Rome. Instead of building from one end to the other, they started in the middle-ish and moved outwards.

Between this, the De-o-Wain-Sta, and the Shadow Gate at Fort Stanwix, Rome is setting on one hell of a crossroads.

I continued reading, out of boredom more than anything, and followed the Blakesley family tree. By the early 1900s, the Lowell Pack had grown to a considerable size, mostly because they kept to themselves as dairy farmers and copper mill workers. They eventually absorbed three other main branches of families, including the Blakesleys. And they were all very well off, hence why Walter accused Henry of being a gold-digger. Even without the possible inheritance, Clara's family was rich.

But they had a string of bad luck back in the 90s. Several random family members passed away from congenital issues. And Clara's mother, Ivy, disappeared. She was a werewolf too, so it seemed odd she'd run away from her pack. But she married into the Lowell pack so her loyalty might have been compromised. She was originally from a pack based just outside...

"Hey, Ryan, you ever heard of King of Prussia?"

"I'm sure it had a king," he replied as he scraped at the bottom of his plastic yogurt cup. "I'm going to guess Frederick."

"No, I mean, King of Prussia, it's a town in Pennsylvania."

Ryan paused, spoon halfway to his mouth. "Who names a town King of Prussia?

"That's what I'm asking you." I left the 'duh' unsaid.

"You're the one with Google." Ryan did not leave the 'duh' unsaid. He said it rather loudly in fact.

"Phil has my phone!"

"Details!"

"We're leaving," Phil announced, walking into the room.

"We are?" Ryan asked.

"We're going to the Blakesley house," Phil clarified. "We're going to meet up with Clara and see what evidence they have on Henry and if we can't find any of our own."

"Phil." I sighed and held my hand over my heart. "I say this from a place of love, but please, don't be me."

Ryan let out some kind of strangled noise before slapping his hand over his mouth. Phil gave me another look that I'm pretty sure he stole from me. This was starting to become a troublesome trend, because *I* am a troublesome trend.

"You're already on Longtree's shit list," I pointed out. "If you start mucking around with evidence and witnesses, it could hamper Henry's case."

Phil cross his arms. "There won't be a case if we can sort this out before it's even started."

"Dude." I nearly threw my hands up. "This is me saying we should slow down and think this through. Me. That should tell you everything."

"I know what I'm doing. Stay here if you want to, but I'd rather you came with us." Phil seemed to assume Ryan was on board with his plan. A glance in Ryan's direction showed the kid trying to be indifferent.

"You only want me to come to be a magic sink." I was more testy than usual about the subject.

"Well, yes, but…" and he stumbled.

"But?" I know what I'm capable of, and I know what my limitations are. I'm useful, but I'm a tool, not a detective.

"Mom, Dad, please don't fight," Ryan chimed in.

We turned to him and that little shit just grinned at us.

"You're lucky you're adorable," I told him.

"I know," he replied, still grinning.

"Minni." Phil was tired. "This is my brother. I won't risk the evidence but I'm not going to sit here and wait, either."

At this point, I didn't think I had much of a choice. Phil's my friend. Sometimes I'm not sure why, or if it's even a good idea, but that's just how it is. And family makes you stupid, one way or another. If anything, someone needed to keep an eye on Phil so he didn't, well, pull a me.

"Alright, fine." I sighed and gestured for Phil to give me my phone. "But you're paying me back for the Lyft charges."

"Don't worry." Ryan stood up. "I got a cheaper idea."

And that is how Phil and I found ourselves standing awkwardly outside in the cold as Ryan leaned against the patrol car, arms crossed on top of the open window.

"I mean, it just makes sense," he said to the uniformed policeman. "You have to watch Phil, Phil needs a lift. You're going to have to drive there anyway. This way we carpool. Help out the environment."

Crickets, I swear to god that was all that we could hear as the cop just looked at Ryan with the most astonished expression. And, well, Ryan wasn't wrong. I guess the cop thought the same thing. That or he appreciated Ryan's ballsy-ness and figured he needed to be rewarded. So he hit the locks and gestured for us to climb into the back.

And that is how we came to have ourselves escorted to the Blakesley house in the back of a patrol car. But Ryan was right—it was cheaper than a ride share.

The house was pretty darn nice, and probably older than my home state of Nebraska. It was three stories of colonial glory. Red brick, actual working shutters, and more character than the McCallister's house. The paperwork I scanned told me I should expect as much, but it's another thing to be confronted by it.

A woman about Phil's age, maybe a little older, opened the door. I tried not to stare at her hair. It was thick and black, but there were layers of natural grey in it that shouldn't really be on someone so young, or someone without a thyroid condition. But she is a werewolf, and that type of coloring reminded me of a Border Collie. Though I suspect it wouldn't have been polite to point that out.

"Phil," she said with only a small manor of relief.

"Hey, Clara. You doing okay?"

"Managing, thank you." She moved to the side and we walked into the entry hall.

The inside had a distinct lack of open concept. It kind of reminded me of Drake's house in Wales, only a bit smaller and a little less Regency. And no pool portals. I hoped.

"Clara," Phil started introductions. "These are friends of mine. This is Minni and Ryan."

"Hello." She tried to smile but ultimately looked too worried and distraught to do much more than move a few facial muscles. "Have you spoken to Henry?"

"No," Phil admitted with a slight side eye at me. "James Masterson has gone down the station to see what he can do."

"That's something at least." Clara sighed. "Gerald was here earlier. I don't know what he's up to, but it can't be good."

"We ran into him as well," Phil said. "He wanted to check my innocence since I was a viable suspect."

"Because of course he did." Clara rolled her eyes which were puffy with a red tint. I was still distracted by her hair. I was wondering if Stacey knew a stylist who could replicate the look. She probably did. It's Stacey after all.

"Can you tell me more about what happened?" Phil asked.

"Yes, of course, and where are my manners?" Clara led us into the living room which had the kind of furniture that was likely made for looking at, not sitting on.

Ryan, Phil, and I sat on a… what's a fancy word for a sofa? Because I'm pretty sure this thing had some kind of fancy French name or something.

Anyway, we sat there as Clara gave us the details of the crime, what she had pieced together from Gerald, Longtree, and a couple of others. It all started after Phil was forcefully ejected from a party at Walter Blakesley's house down the road. It had been some kind of watch party for the super blood blue moon.

The party ended and a bunch of them decided to go out into the woods to change and run. Walter stayed back, and an hour later Gerald discovered him in the back yard, stabbed with a silver dagger. Which is like, overkill.

Seriously, when a werewolf is in their human form, they are still stronger and have better senses than the average human, but they are by no means invincible. Any old sharp instrument would have done him in if applied properly to the task; it didn't have to be silver.

Henry would have known that.

The theory of the crime was Walter and Henry got into it over both Phil and the fact Walter was trying to stop Henry from joining the pack. The dagger was part of a cutlery set that dated back to when Revere Copper started producing copper-clad cookware back in like, the '30s. So, actually, Walter was killed by an over-sharp butter knife.

It wasn't even in use. It was in a display case in the living room, which is past the kitchen. I know because I asked. Because if we're talking about a weapon of convenience, it surely wasn't convenient. Not when passing a kitchen full of sharper objects.

The cops believed Henry was in too much of a blind rage to think things through logically. Not sure I agree. I've been in a blind rage, and I grabbed the closest weapon available. Then I beat the ever-loving shit out of the subject of said rage.

Cold and calculating murder came later.

It seemed to me, with my expertise from years of watching police procedurals, that the motive and modus operandi didn't match up. Walter's death was far more deliberate than what Longtree presumed it to be.

"So," Ryan said when the conversation went quiet, "other than the 'motive', what does Longtree have on Henry?"

"Sorry?" Clara frowned.

"It's too soon for fingerprints or DNA to come back," Ryan pointed out. "And the body probably hasn't even been removed from the scene yet. The only way a cop is going to arrest someone so quickly is if they have some pretty damning evidence."

Well, he's not wrong.

"Henry didn't murder anyone," Phil quickly defended.

"I'm not saying he did!" Ryan inched away from Phil and into me. "But Henry was *arrested*, not brought in for questioning. Longtree started the clock on needing to press charges. Why do that unless you're pretty confident in knowing who the killer is?"

"Clara?" Phil turned to her.

"I don't know." She shook her head. "I wasn't here when it happened. I was at Aunt Lori's. She lives across from Walter and had a bit of a fright. I was walking back when Henry was put in the police car."

Phil got that pensive look on his face, deep in thought. It was good to see him looking a bit more like himself.

The front door opened and Clara sniffed at the air. A man with similar hair, though cut rather short, walked into the room. He was significantly more tired looking, his face a little gaunt. He glanced around at us with a wary eye.

"This is my brother, Luke," Clara introduced him. "Luke, this is Phil, Henry's brother. I don't think you've met yet."

"I don't believe we have," Luke said and offered his hand.

Phil stood and shook it, then gestured to us. "This is Ryan and Minni, friends of mine."

"Friends?" Luke frowned, pointing vaguely at me. "She's the, what? Niece of the probate lawyer?"

"How did you…?" I was suitably dumbfounded.

"You have a very similar sent," Luke explained. "There is a strange undercurrent of metallics that can only be familial."

I glanced down at my bracelet. "What?"

"Luke is very hypersensitive," Clara spoke as if she was apologizing. "Even for a werewolf, he can smell things most of us can't."

"Sorry," Luke did apologize. "I didn't think. I'm a bit… rattled right now, with everything…"

"It's fine." Not like it was a big secret James is my Uncle.

Luke turned to his sister. "The coroner just left Walter's along with the forensic techs. They released the crime scene."

"They did?" Phil asked.

"Yes, they said something about no point in roping off a backyard in the middle of winter." Luke explained. "Between the snow and general elements, won't be much to find."

A general murmur of agreement went around the room before Phil asked, "What about Henry? Did they say why he was arrested?"

"Yeah, he, ah," Luke got really cagey and glanced at his sister. "He confessed."

And gone was the calm and thoughtful coven-leader.

The next ten minutes was just a lot of noise, most of it I didn't understand, like, at all.

"He didn't do it," Luke said, eventually getting both Clara and Phil to just stop. "I could smell it on him. I don't know why he confessed, but he didn't do it."

"That's not going to convince Longtree," Ryan helpfully pointed out. He then regretted his decision as soon as Phil and Clara both glared at him.

"I'm going to call Dad," Clara said, grabbing her phone from the coffee table.

"They're all still on the deep run," Luke said.

"Deep run?" I asked because I always get stuck on the weirdest things.

"The pack runs deep into the Sand Plains. It's, ah, a pine forest to the west," Luke explained. "They will be gone for hours. They don't know what happened to Walter."

That made me blink. "So, wait, there's a whole pack of wolves who are going to run back into town and discover one of their patriarchs is dead?"

Clara snorted. "Walter was no patriarch. He was a bully."

"Clara." Luke pre-emptively tried to calm her down.

"I know he's only been dead a couple of hours now, but I'm not going to pretend he wasn't a grade-a asshole." Clara was flustered and she might have even growled. "It's a miracle Aunt Lori didn't kick him out of the pack years ago."

"Could she have done that?" I asked.

"Yes," Clara answered adamantly.

"Aunt Lori is pack mother of the Blakesley sub-pack," Luke explained before I could ask for clarification. "Walt could appeal to Georgina Lowell, the den mother, but generally she will side with her chosen pack mothers. She wouldn't promote them if she didn't think she could trust their judgements."

In the past two hours I learned more about werewolf politics and pack dynamics than I ever really wanted to know. At that point, a surprise visit by a certain annoying dragon might actually have been welcomed. But I'm glad I paid attention, or at least remembered enough. Because sometimes I surprise myself.

There was frantic knocking on the door. Luke went to it and must have smelt who was on the other side because he opened it without even looking. A man about my age came rushing in, his breath quick and eyes a little wide. I remembered him as being one of the guys hanging out with Gerald earlier.

"Clara, Luke," he said as if relieved to see them.

"What is it, Declan?" Luke asked.

A hallway clock began chiming twelve bells for midnight.

Declan swallowed hard. "There's been another murder."

Okay, that one I didn't see coming.

EIGHT[8]

Wednesday, January 31st, 2018
12:00am

"What?" Clara sputtered. "Another murder?"

"Who?" Luke asked the burning question.

"Aunt Lori," Declan answered as he caught his breath.

"Aunt Lori?" Clara whispered like she was in pain. Her knees buckled and Luke grabbed her shoulders to steady her.

"What happened?" Phil asked.

"She overdosed on her nightly heart medication," Declan explained. "At first we thought it might have been an accident, but we smelled the medicine. Crushed up and diluted in her water glass."

"Wouldn't she have smelt it, too?" Phil questioned as he helped Luke guide Clara to the sofa.

"Aunt Lori had a stroke a few years back, lost most of her sense of smell. Anyway, the police have been called, they should be arriving soon." Declan gestured helplessly. "Just thought you should know."

Clara sat down on the sofa, putting her head in her hands. "What is going on? It's like the world's gone mad!"

I was actually wondering if I was still in bed and having a very vivid nightmare-adjacent dream. I show up in town and two people die. It usually comes in threes, so now I was seriously worrying about the health and safety of everyone in said town. It's not that I think of myself as a bad luck charm, but got to look at the facts here…

Sirens sounded in the distance and we all went outside, because… reasons? I honestly had no idea what to do at that point. Everything was escalating so quickly. My go-to reaction of just zapping the problem wasn't going to work this time.

Gerald and his crew were standing out in the street in front of what I assume was Aunt Lori's house. An ambulance arrived along with a few cop cars. Detective Longtree exited from one of them and Phil made a beeline to him.

"This isn't the time, Mr. McCree," Longtree said as he tried to skirt past Phil.

"I don't care what Henry said!" Phil is a wizard, he could do stubborn. Maybe not as well as me, but adequately enough. "He didn't murder anyone."

"I'm not discussing an ongoing investigation." Longtree was going to arrest Phil just for annoying him, I could feel it.

"Hey, Phil," I quickly moved forward and grabbed his arm. "Look at the moon, isn't it pretty?"

"Huh?" He was so completely thrown by that, glancing up at the sky as if it might be falling. This allowed Longtree to move past and towards the house. When it clicked with Phil what happened, he was a bit cross with me. "Why did you do that?"

"Because apparently I'm the adult now," I shot back. "And that's not a good thing!"

"She's right, you know." Ryan, always so helpful. "Minni doesn't adult well and you should know better. Why am I the one saying this?"

Phil looked at us like we were traitors.

"Face the facts, Phil," I tried to say softly, "this isn't a magic thing. Sure, werewolves are involved, but that's it." I gestured to all the very normal, mundane, police cars and emergency vehicles. "If it wasn't for that, this would just be another case of rich white family drama."

"Excuse me?" Gerald was downright scandalized.

"That's right, I said it," I called back at him. "I bet you, dollars to donuts, that this is about money."

"Don't you mean dollars to munchkins?" Ryan asked.

Gerald stalked over to us. "Uncle Walt, unlike his brother, died with a will. It leaves everything to Clara and Luke's father, who is still up in the woods." He looked directly at Phil. "Seems like a good motive for your brother."

Good thing I still had a hold of Phil because he did start to lurch forward. Me having to be the responsible one was getting really old. I can only adult so much until I'm like, `fuck it,' and I just let everything burn to the ground.

Um, too soon?

"Don't be an idiot," I said to both idiots, then specifically addressed Gerald. "Killing Walter gives Clara's dad the money, not Clara. And if Henry killed Walt in order to get in line for the money faster, why would he confess?"

Gerald blinked at that. "He confessed?"

"That's what he said." I pointed at Luke.

Luke looked startled for a moment, standing in the back of the group. "I didn't actually hear him confess. That's just what I heard the policemen say as they left."

"So, what I'm hearing," I said before everything got loud again, "is that no one knows exactly what is going on here and we should all just chill."

"Can we not chill?" Ryan asked. "Because it's flipping cold out here. Can we go back inside?"

We managed to get everyone ushered to Clara's house—or, well, her father's house actually. Clara and Luke still lived there because, you know, pack animals.

Unfortunately, moving into where it was warm did little to calm or quiet all the parties involved. Everyone kept throwing around motives and explanations and theories. Gerald seemed to think only marginally better of Henry than Walt had, so he had some choice words to say. It started to get petty and I was a hundred percent sure Phil was going to haul off and punch Gerald.

I took a deep breath and concentrated on feeling all the static electricity in the room. It's always there, but usually goes unnoticed until it builds up to the point that it will spark. With the snow outside and the fire indoors, there was just enough humidity in the air to make electrical conductivity that much easier.

All I had to do was nudge some electronics and… *zap!*

A chorus of yelps filled the room as everyone received a small static discharge courtesy of my innate ability to control energy. Of course, only two of the people in the room knew that.

"Dude!" Ryan yelled indignantly at me as he rubbed his leg where the charge hit. "What did I do?"

"It was an area of effect spell."

"You did that?" Gerald asked, his short hair sticking up slightly.

"Yes, to get all y'all's attention." I crossed my arms and tried to look commanding. Which is laughable, I know. "First off, if you don't calm your asses down and behave like adults, I will tase all of you, indiscriminately."

"I'm just gonna go hang out in the other room," Ryan said.

"Secondly, I told you: if Walter didn't have a wife or a mistress, then this has got to be about the money." I looked straight at Gerald. "So, tell us about the money."

NINE[9]

"I'm being robbed."

"What?" Minni asked as Phil stopped in front of her, nearly causing a collision.

"Someone's here," he replied quietly.

They just walked in through the back door of the Mercury Shop after a short trip to Boston via the nearby Shadow Gate. Phil had started a habit of asking Minni along on his adventures, typically for the same reason: to be a magic sink. This time, Minni had spent most of the trip playing Tetris on her phone. She was still playing the game when they entered the shop.

"Okay, more description please." Minni tucked her phone away, scanning the room.

"My things have been moved," he explained in a near whisper as he slowly walked forward. Minni could feel his magic reaching out, scanning for anything else out of place.

Nothing looked off to Minni, but she would be the first to admit she has very poor spatial awareness. Instead, she reached out as well, touching the wards surrounding the building. They were still up, and at full force. She asked quietly, "Maybe Eli or Viv stopped by? Who else has a key? Arid?"

"No, well, yes. But I'd know if it was them." Phil stopped at the curtain that divided the back room from the store proper. He looked at Minni and tilted his head towards the front.

Minni moved forward, taking light steps. She reached out to sense anything amiss and came up with nothing. But it was the kind of nothing that shouldn't exist, like opening up a window and being surprised not to hear the sounds of traffic or birds. She pumped magic into her focus bracelet as Phil silently slid his blasting rod from his satchel.

"You ready?" he mouthed.

Minni nodded yes.

Phil did a silent count of one, two, three, and then they were through the curtain. There was plenty of light streaming in from the streetlamps shinning through the large front windows. It made it all that easier to spot the shadow that moved, darting from the bookcase. The intruder was small, hiding easily in the deeper shadows of the display tables.

"Whoever you are," Phil called out, "it would be better for you to show yourself."

Nothing but silence answered him.

"Look, you're trapped in here." Phil took a few steps forward, past the sales counter, and Minni stayed back to guard the doorway. "I don't want to hurt you. I'm sure we can come to a reasonable—"

A flash of light, like a white-hot flare, erupted in the room. It would temporarily blind a normal person, instantly bleaching their rhodopsin into translucency, taking minutes to recover. Most wizards knew how to block a flare as it was an easy attack spell. Not having a readied defense would be like leaving the house without pants on. Which is why hardly anyone bothered to use it anymore, because it wouldn't do much to a magic user with even the smallest amount of training.

But it might give the intruder the split-second they needed to get out the front door.

Minni had already regained back most of her sight when she saw the figure working the lock of the door whilst knocking down the ward. Not wanting to risk using lightning because of all the flammable things in the shop, she resorted to a more mundane form of offense. She grabbed a hefty tin of chamomile tea from the sales counter, and chucked it across the room, hitting the person squarely between the shoulder blades. They stumbled into the door with a yelp.

"Don't try that again," Phil said as he was now a few feet from the intruder, blasting rod extended. "I'll fire blindly but I can't miss at this range."

They got the hint, holding up their hands in defeat.

"Turn around, slowly," Phil told them.

The intruder did as he said, slowly turning around to reveal themselves to be a teenage boy. He had jet black hair that looked like it'd been cut short with a pair of likely rusted scissors. The t-shirt he wore probably hadn't been washed in weeks, perhaps months. He had a black athletic bag slung over one shoulder. But what stood out the most was how gaunt and tired he appeared.

Phil didn't waver, his blasting rod still at the ready, only his tone changing. "What's your name?"

He almost didn't answer, glancing between both of them with suspicion. Eventually he stumbled out the word, "Ryan."

"Okay, Ryan, can you help me understand what's going on here?"

Minni got the impression the kid didn't trust them. But then again, he didn't look like he trusted anyone so they shouldn't take it personally.

"You're Phil, right?" he finally asked.

"I am. And this is my shop."

"I, ah, I needed some supplies," Ryan began to explain, not exactly apologetic. "Was told this is the place to go. But you weren't here so… yeah."

"How did you get past my ward without breaking it?"

"I told it I was a rabbit."

Minni let out a short bark of laughter. Both men looked at her with wildly juxtaposed expressions. "You got to admit, Phil, that's pretty clever."

"And not easy to do," Phil agreed, turning back to the kid. "How'd you do it?"

Ryan shrugged. "Locks talk, you just have to listen."

Phil considered this for a moment, then lowered his blasting rod. "When was the last time you ate, Ryan?"

This sent a new flood of suspicion through him. "Why?"

"Because you look like you're starving," Phil answered bluntly which didn't make things any better.

"Hey," Minni spoke up. "You came here for help, right? For supplies and whatnot? That's because Phil is good at helping people. Think it through, man."

Ryan frowned, but fixed his bag, making it sturdier on his shoulder. "Food sounds good."

Phil slid his blasting rod back into his satchel. "I think the Chinese place is still open for delivery. You like Chinese?"

"Dumplings!" he said rather quickly. "Um, please."

"Just dumplings?" Phil asked him.

"Lots of dumplings?"

"Okay, ah, Minni, would you do the honors?" Phil asked and Minni started going through her contacts to find the number.

There was a wary silence between everyone, even as Minni ordered the food. Ryan looked like he still didn't trust them, but perhaps twenty-five percent less than he did before.

"Who told you about me?" Phil asked.

Ryan got defensive again. "I hear things, here and there."

Phil didn't push any further on that subject. "I hope they explained what I do. This city has no offices for any of the New England Wizards Councils. I created this shop so that wizards would have a safe space to come if they were in need."

"Yeah, that's the word," Ryann mumbled, glancing around so he wouldn't be looking at us. Phil would have given him all of the supplies he needed, had he waited and asked properly, and Ryan seemed to have realized this possibly a tad bit too late.

"While we wait, Ryan, there's a shower upstairs, and I have some clean clothes you can have," Phil offered, and Ryan looked only moderately suspicious of the offer. "Why don't you clean yourself up? We'll eat, then we can look into contacting your parents to—"

"No!" Ryan nearly shouted, his voice going high-pitched.

"What's wrong?"

"You contact my parents and they're going to want me to come home," Ryan looked absolutely terror stricken at the idea, eyes gone wide and body trembling. "And I can't... I can't go home. Just let me leave, I'll never come back here, I promise."

Phil frowned at Ryan, his brow crinkling as he attempted to understand the situation. Then his expression softened. "Okay. We won't contact your parents for the time being. But I'm still not letting you go back out there without a proper meal and some supplies."

There was a good minute where Minni thought Ryan was going to try to bolt on them again. But if Ryan had found Phil's shop because others talked about him, then he would know that Phil was one of the good guys. That Phil could be trusted.

"Thanks," Ryan said just loud enough to be heard.

Phil took Ryan upstairs to the small apartment Minni had used while she waited at the front for the food delivery. Phil came back down after leaving Ryan to shower and change.

"That kid looks like he's had it rough," Minni commented as Phil started to put his things away from their trip.

"He has," Phil agreed. "I'll let him stay for a bit, long enough to get him on his feet."

Three weeks later and Ryan was still there.

"Hey, Ryan," Minni said as she entered the shop to see the kid sitting behind the counter, feet propped up, reading a book. "Where's Phil?"

"Had to pop over to Connecticut. A coven up there needed a helping hand for a big spell."

"Oh, okay." Minni was unsure what to make of this news. She supposed whatever he was doing didn't need her special skill set. She'd grown used to Phil asking her to help out, be a magic sink. As much as it annoyed her that this was all she was useful for, at least she was useful.

"He said you'd be by." Ryan turned a page in the book. "Said he'd count you as checked in for the week."

"Thanks." At least that was one thing Minni didn't have to worry about. She knew Phil sent reports to the councils, but she didn't know what was in them, or how much they paid attention to them. They hadn't said anything about her using magic on the camazotz, or the dozen-ish other times since. But then something occurred to her. "Wait, Phil left you in charge of the shop?"

"Yep."

Minni pouted. "I lived up there for just as long, longer even, and he never asked me to cover the shop."

Ryan glanced up from his book. "I've known you three weeks and even I know you should never be left in charge of anything. You don't adult well."

"Hate you a little bit right now."

"Only because I'm right."

"Yeah, that's fair." Minni nodded sagely.

Two weeks after this moment where Minni subconsciously decided to adopt Ryan as a younger brother, she was back in the shop for her weekly visit.

"Prisoner two-four-six-oh-one reporting in," Minni said as she walked up to the counter.

Phil was writing something in his ledger, but paused long enough to give Minni the most dour of expressions.

"It's Ginny's favorite movie right now," Minni defended herself. "She keeps playing it over and over. I can probably sing the entire soundtrack. Horribly off key, but I could."

"I'll take your word for it." Phil managed to cover most of his chuckle.

Ryan walked in from the back. "Oh, hey Minni."

"Hey." She gave a little half wave.

"Phil," Ryan turned to him. "Where's the scissors?"

"Cutting paper or fabric?" Phil asked.

"Hair, specifically, mine."

"Use the blue handled pair, middle shelf in the back, probably behind the exorcism kit."

"Thanks!" Ryan said as he went to leave.

"Hold up." Minni stopped him. "You're going to cut your own hair?"

Ryan seemed to think it was a trick question on her part and eyed her warily. "Uh, yeah."

"No, we're finding you a proper barber." Minni pulled out her phone and sent off a text to her roommate, Stacey. *"Hey, it's Minni. I have a fashion emergency. Got a friend who needs a haircut."*

"It's fine." Ryan tried to wave her off. "I'm not trying to impress anyone or anything."

"Your hair looks like it's been stuck in a weedwhacker," Minni replied bluntly.

"Gee, thanks." Ryan's tone indicated the opposite.

"How fast can you be at this address?" Stacey texted Minni.

"Twenty minutes," Minni sent, then slid her phone in her back pocket. "Okay, we need to get to the subway."

"I'm not sure this is a good idea." Ryan was almost timid.

"Just, trust me. Getting a proper haircut will make you feel like a new man."

"Um, Minni?" Phil ventured into the conversation, then stalled out when she looked at him.

"What?" Minni asked, then she thought it through. "Oh, yeah, well, I'll pay for it. It's my idea. Think of it as, ah, an early Christmas present."

Phil tilted his head slightly, as if realizing they weren't on the same page.

Ryan cleared his throat. "You know what? A proper haircut does sound good. Haven't had one in ages. And if you're going to foot the bill, I'll trust you."

Minni snorted. "Okay, that's your first mistake. But my roommate, you can trust her. There is very little she takes more seriously than fashion."

Twenty minutes later, Minni and Ryan met Stacey outside of a Dunkin, hot coffee in hand to ward off the chill in the air.

"This is Ryan," Minni introduced him. "He works for my friend Phil at his shop."

"Nice to meet you." Stacey was bright and personable, then turned a critical eye on him. "Now, do you know what you're wanting? Do you have a style in mind?"

Ryan rocked nervously on his feet. "I was thinking maybe something like Dylan O'Brien?"

"Perfect." Stacey grinned. "I know exactly where to go."

Two blocks over was a salon. Everyone greeted Stacey as if she was an old friend. Minni figured she probably was. So she let

Stacey do her thing in getting Ryan set up with a stylist. Minni flopped down in a chair and picked up one of the magazines.

"He's in good hands," Stacey said as she sat down beside her, leaving the stylist to do their work and not hovering.

"I didn't think he wasn't," Minni replied, flipping through the magazine, barely scanning the articles.

"It's funny you should think that, since you never say more than five words to me." She turned halfway in her seat, her elbow resting on the back. "You never say more than five words to any of us."

Minni shrugged. "Don't take it personally."

"Oh, I never take anything personally," she laughed. "Bad for one's complexion."

"There you go then." Minni turned to a new page and kept pretending she was reading and comprehending whatever sage advice the magazine was trying to extoll.

"Being an introvert, I get, but you… you are no introvert." Stacey tilted her head slightly, as if she could read Minni's aura. But Stacey didn't have any magic. "You just don't want to make any friends."

"I am a shitty friend," Minni replied so quickly it was everything she could do not to wince.

Stacey made a herm sound. "Yet, here you are, sitting in a salon on a Saturday, helping someone you've only known a few weeks feel better about themselves."

"It's just a haircut."

"Yeah, yeah it is, just a haircut." Stacey spoke as if she had stumbled onto something very profound. If Stacey was trying to get under Minni's skin, then she had done a primo job of it.

"How do I look?" Ryan asked when the stylist let him out of the chair.

"Well, you no longer look like you got your head stuck in a weedwhacker, so, progress," Minni answered honestly causing Stacey to face-palm.

"You realize you're paying for this." Ryan pointed at his hair. "Literally."

"Yeah, I should probably do that." Minni stood up and walked over to the counter. She paid for the cut, tipped rather well, and ignored the fact that Stacey was right.

Minni was beginning to learn that Stacey usually is.

TEN[10]

November 13th, 2013

It wasn't often that Minni visited the Financial District. She actively avoided it, if she was honest with herself. The area just felt grimy, and that was without her reaching out with her third eye. As she walked down the street, the sun having disappeared behind the buildings of Lower Manhattan, she skirted around a small crowd taking pictures of the Charging Bull.

Turning down one of the alleys, she found a door just as the message described. She tried the handle. Unlocked, as promised. She was met by darkness and a dead light switch. After a moment of hesitation, she turned on her phone's flashlight instead of resorting to magic. It would be easier to explain should she run into anyone other than the person she was there to meet.

Paint peeled off the hallway walls, and there was a slight musk to the air.

"Not creepy at all," she mumbled as she moved forward.

Two lefts and a right, that's what the message had said. Dutifully, she followed the directions. The second left took her into a better maintained area with offices lining each side. There were a lot of acronyms after the names, none of which she really understood. The right took her down a hall that was starker in comparison. All it had was a singular door at the end and a teenager sitting against the wall.

"Minni." Ryan stood up quickly. "Glad you got my send."

"You're lucky I was in my room." Minni pointed the phone-light down so it would defuse across the pale walls and not blind them. "Your note said you were stuck, needed a degauss?"

"Yeah, right there." Ryan turned sideways and pointed to the electric lock on the far door. "I got the cameras and the alarm, but I've built up too much magic. I touch that thing and it'll fry."

"Easy enough fix." Minni walked past him, syphoning off his magic buildup as she did so.

Everyone's aura is unique, but magic itself is all the same. It gains it's colors, textures, and tastes from the person who holds the magic in their aura. The magical static that builds up around the aura is like a watered down version. It offers a hint of the wizard's aura, a leftover filmy residue. It wants to be part of something again, it wants to connect, so it clings to the wizard in hopes of somehow being reabsorbed into the aura.

Ryan's felt cold and solid, smelt of the sea air and tasted of salt. It represented an interesting dichotomy because the young man did not like seafood of any kind. He also didn't care for the beach, lamenting that sitting around, sweating under the cancer-giving sun was not his idea of fun.

The briny static that built up around his aura was in need of a place to harbor, and it took no effort for Minni to entice it to her own aura. It poured in, siphoning through to rid itself of the auric residue that he contained to meld with Minni's magic. For her part, she only felt a light brush of air tickling the hairs on the back of her neck.

Reaching the keypad, some magic had seeped into it, but it was nothing for her to clear it. She touched the magic with her aura, inviting it to join. Like Ryan's auric static, it found Minni's offer to be far too enticing to pass up. It always did.

"There you go," she said when she was done.

"You're awesome." Ryan went to the keypad and punched in numbers that were written on his left palm. "I'll buy you Dunkin when we're done here."

"I'll hold you to that." The door popped open and Minni glanced around, the pieces falling into place. Or at least a few them. The rest had been knocked to the floor. "Um, Ryan. What exactly are you doing here?"

Ryan paused, door half opened. "What does it look like?"

"You're... robbing the place?" The statement came out as awkward as Minni suddenly felt.

"I am not." Ryan tsked. "This a B&E, without the B."

"Oh…" Minni took a deep breath. "What?"

"Here. I'll show you." Ryan gestured for her to follow him inside the room. The lights didn't work in there either, so Ryan created a small ball of defused light and stuck it to the ceiling. Examination of the room showed it to be some kind of file storage. The fact that it was under lock spoke volumes towards the information held in the file cabinets that lined in rows.

"How long until I count as an accessory?" Minni asked. "Or have I blown right passed that?"

"I said I wasn't stealing anything," he sounded a tad bit offended. But was it because she accused him of stealing, or because he wasn't going to steal something? "Just looking for some information."

"I probably shouldn't ask, but what information?"

"You know Arid, right?" Ryan said as he started to open cabinets. "Two kids, normal husband, good at potions?"

"Everyone knows Arid," Minni pointed out.

"Well, the bank is trying to take their house."

"What?" Minni laughed. It had to be a joke of some kind.

Ryan closed a drawer and opened another. "Someone in this office did something hinky. Accounts aren't adding up. I'm looking for proof. Something I can tell Arid's lawyers to look for."

"Oh…" The word came out a little sullen. "That's… probably still illegal but, yeah, happy to help."

"Figured you would be." He gave a know-it-all-grin.

Minni rolled her eyes and looked around the room with this new perspective. There were lots and lots of file cabinets with banker's boxes stacked on top. "What are we looking for?"

"I'll know it when I see it." Ryan gestured to the cabinet he was working through. "These are all the loan documents."

"Right, well…" Minni spotted a small desk with rolly chair. She sat down, spun around once for good measure, and then settled herself to wait. Ryan might need her to drain his magic again in order to put everything back the way he left it. "Just let me know if you need me to do anything."

"Will do," he said, flipping through a file.

Minni pulled out her phone, playing some game or another to keep herself occupied. But after a couple of minutes, it was clear her heart wasn't in it. Nor was her head, which she was hoping to dull with some mindless pattern matching. Stacey's comments just kept scratching away at her until it was a loud roaring in her ears.

"You don't want to make friends," Stacey had told her, then heavily implied that Minni did so anyway…

"Hey, Minni," Ryan got her attention.

"You find it?"

"Not yet." Ryan had several files spread out around him on the floor. "But it occurred to me, you never finished telling your story."

Minni frowned. "What story?"

"The Copper Knight. You started telling it the other day at the shop but then that customer came in and they just…" Ryan tapped his thumb and fingers together in a talky gesture.

"Oh yeah." Minni remembered now. "I could tell it to you, if you're still interested?"

"Was then, still am." He smiled and urged her to continue.

"Well, I barely got started." Minni's memory of the day was a little hazy. "I'll just start from the beginning, if that's okay?"

"Sure." He held up a file. "I may be looking at this but I'm listening. I multi-task really well."

"That makes one of us." Minni snorted, then took a second to gather her thoughts. "Okay, so the story goes back to sometime in the Dark Ages. There was a small kingdom that doesn't exist anymore, but that's getting ahead of the story. Point is, there was a King, he had a Knight, and the land was being threatened by other kingdoms."

"What other kingdoms?" Ryan asked.

"Huh?"

"Are we talking like, Prussia?" He paused, glancing up as if the answer was written somewhere above Minni's head. "Wait, were the Prussians around in the Dark Ages? Who was in charge in the Dark Ages? Anyone? Was that the point?"

Minni stared blankly at him. "I think you're reading far too much into this. It's just a story."

"But it's supposed to have happened, right?"

"Supposedly." Minni did not speak with confidence. "It's a parable, okay?"

"Alright." He frowned, but ignored it. "Continue."

"Let's see, the King, who no, I don't know his name so let's just call him the King, he was trying to find a way to repel his enemies and keep the land safe. He heard rumors of the Book of Gaerwen and that it was somewhere… vaguely… south… ish." Minni realized she was gesturing to a direction that may or may not be south. She pulled her hand back and put it in her lap, hoping Ryan hadn't noticed.

"Book of Gaerwen," Ryan repeated. "He was one of your famous ancestors?"

"Ah, yes, Gaerwen was a Masterson of the Second Son of the First Master. He had long since died but when he was alive, he had befriended some dragons."

"European dragons, right?"

"Yes, European," Minni answered, then thought about it for a second. "I mean, there is nothing to say he didn't meet Asian dragons, though it's very unlikely he met any South American dragons." She made a mental note to ask her mom about that later. "Anyway, he basically learned all their dragon-y secrets and wrote it down in a book."

"As one does," Ryan said poshly.

"As one does." Minni chuckled. "So, the King knows he has a Knight who is a Masterson, although he is of the Fourth Son of the First Master."

Ryan held up his hand. "Which one are you again?"

"Sixth," she answered. "The King sends the Knight to go look for the book. The Knight travels to the southern regions, does some investigating, and it leads him to a quarry town. He's told to speak to a witch on the outskirts. Her name is Vask and she's known to have eclectic things. She also has a dragon familiar, a baby copper dragon named Midi."

"Wait." Ryan held up his hand again. "You don't know the name of the country, the King, or the Knight, but you know the name of the witch and her familiar?"

Minni stared blankly at him. "Does this surprise you?"

After a moment's consideration, Ryan made a 'you may proceed' gesture.

"So, Vask isn't going to hand over the Book of Gaerwen to just anyone," Minni continued. "She doesn't even know this guy. And witches and wizards are, well, notoriously paranoid." She ignored Ryan's snort. "Vask expected the Knight to be brash, maybe try to fight her, or just be super persistent. But he only asks that she hears his story, and if she still says no, then he'll return to the King. She agrees and listens to the Knight speak of his home, his people, etc."

Ryan gave Minni a very perturbed look. "Why do I feel like your next words are going to be 'she fell madly in love with the Knight and handed over the book'?"

"Eh, close." Minni shrugged. "She does tell him no, he can't have the book. He leaves and goes back to the village proper, but he doesn't return to his King. He sticks around and does… whatever knights do when not doing knightly things. I dunno, getting cats out of trees? Juggling swords? Whatever."

"Hold a sec." Ryan held up his hand again, although this time in a halting gesture. He put away some of the folders he was going through and grabbed another set. "Okay, go."

"Vask sees the Knight the next time she ventures into town and asks him why he hadn't returned to his King. He says he promised to return, just didn't say when." Minni paused. "Being a cheeky motherfucker is apparently a Masterson family trait."

Ryan didn't bother to try to cover his bark of laughter.

"Well, the Knight never went back to Vask's hut as promised, but as the village wasn't terribly huge, they saw each other when she came in for supplies. He never asked about the Book of Gaerwen, but they did have conversations." Minni let out a confused sigh. She used to think this was all romantic, but she'd grown up since then. "And yeah, they fall in love."

"You really sold that last part," Ryan said with about as much oomph as Minni had given it.

"My mom is usually the one telling the story," Minni pointed out. "She goes into a lot more detail and… and yeah… I'm giving you *Cliff Notes* version here."

Ryan simply shrugged. "Please continue then."

Minni regathered her thoughts and picked up where she left off. "Okay, so, they fall in love, but the Knight still has his duty to his King who he believes to be a right and honorable man. Vask agrees to give the Knight the book. He promises he will deliver it to the King and then immediately return to her. He makes it back to his kingdom, gives the King the book. Then he does exactly as he said he would: he leaves to return to Vask."

"This doesn't end well, does it?" Ryan asked.

"Hey, don't get ahead of the story," Minni replied drolly. "Now, travel between the King's castle and the quarry village takes several days, so while the Knight is on the road, the King has time to read through the book. He said he was going to find something to help him gain the aid of the dragons. Maybe find something he could trade for their service. Make them a mix-tape, I dunno. Instead, he finds a dragon binding spell."

"This is a specific spell geared towards dragons only, right?" Ryan asked for clarification. "Not an all-purpose binding spell?"

"Yeah, which means it's a lot harder to break, but also, if you set it up right, like merge it into a focus item instead of just casting it, then it won't wear off if you can keep feeding the spell," Minni explained and then trailed off when she realized she probably didn't need to. Not to Ryan anyway. "So the King decides screw diplomacy, he'll just *make* the dragons do his bidding. The Knight returns to Vask at the same time as the King performs the spell which binds all dragons within the space of the Sleeping Moon."

"The what now?"

"It's a fancy way to say the time it takes for the moon to go from new moon to full moon."

He thought about that for a second. "Oh, so like, every dragon within two weeks travel?"

"Pretty much." Although Minni would be the first to admit that her astronomy and astrology classes were not her best.

"So is this foot travel? Dragon travel?" Ryan asked.

"Probably dragon travel, if I had to guess." Minni and her siblings had asked many of the same questions when they were younger and that was what they settled on. "So yeah, the King casts the spell and Vask and Midi are both caught up in it because, surprise, Vask was actually a copper dragon in human form and Midi was actually her daughter."

"I'm just so shocked I never would have guessed," Ryan said with a completely blanked face.

"Hey, when you're not even double digits yet, this story is amaze-balls." Minni paused before adding. "And I should never say amaze-balls, like, ever again."

"Probably a good idea," Ryan agreed.

"Yeah, well, anyway, Vask turns back into her dragon form and flies, with Midi, to the King's castle where he's gotten all the dragons to converge. The Knight immediately follows, but the dragons can fly faster than he can ride a horse. He's a few days behind, and that's enough. The King has several dragons bound to him now and he sets them against the other kingdoms, the results being, well..." Minni made several explosion sounds, miming with her hands.

She cleared her throat and continued. "The Knight sees this and is horrified, of course. This is not what he signed up for by giving the King the book. And he tells him that, to his face."

"I bet that went over well," Ryan said wryly.

"The King decides to put the Knight to death for... what's the old-timey word for insubordination?"

"Why are you asking me?" Ryan frowned at her. "It's your mom's story. What word did she use?"

"I can't remember it, okay?" Minni huffed. "Whatever, it's not important. What *is* important is that the King's method of execution is 'death by dragon.'"

Ryan's eyes went a little rounder and for the first time showed a hint of fear and worry. "He's going to make Vask kill her boyfriend?"

"No, of course not," she assured him, not realizing he had gotten that invested in the story. "The King doesn't know about the relationship, and copper dragons spit acid which is not flashy at all. Now, gold dragons, they are fire-breathers. And there just happens to be a gold one in the group. So, before he's executed, the King asks the Knight if he has any last words, and he does: *Oh, were I to learn sooner, there is no such thing as a good man, only an evil one who understands that everyone else is as important as they are.*"

"That's..." Ryan got a bit thoughtful, scratching at his temple. "That's a load of horseshit."

All Minni could do was shrug. She had spent many an hour thinking about this part of the tale as a child. It haunted her after she took a life to save her brother. "It's just a story."

"It's your family's story," Ryan pointed out softly.

Minni didn't refute Ryan's comment. The Legend of the Copper Knight had been passed through her family for years. Well, her father's side, the Masterson's side. But it was her mother who would tell it to Minni and her siblings, often as a bedtime story. On more than one occasion the Masterson children could be found running around the backyard, acting out the legend, or at least the battles. Sometimes they would ask their mom to tell it so she'd be distracted as another sibling did something that would warrant a wooden spoon across the knuckles.

"It's still just a story," Minni said, pain bubbling up from places better left undisturbed since that night in the sunflower field.

Ryan got the hint, quickly sorting through another stack of papers. "So, a gold dragon was about to french-fry the Knight?"

"Yeah, ah." Minni cleared her throat again. "That's what the King wanted. But what's the major flaw in binding spells?"

"Interpretation," Ryan answered immediately. "When you give a command it needs to be specific or else the bound subject can interpret it any way they choose to."

"Exactly. And in this case, the King said *burn him*, which, sounds straight forward…" Minni allowed herself a small grin, she always did like this part. "Now, Vask had told the other dragons about the Knight, and obviously they saw the Knight truly regretted giving the King the book, so the gold dragon does burn the Knight. Burns him just enough around the middle to make the ropes tying him to the post… Wait, did I mention he was tied to a post?"

"No, but I assumed," Ryan said.

"Right, okay, so the ropes are burned through. The Knight only suffers minor damage. Nothing that stops him from getting the hell out of Dodge." Minni took a second to form her thoughts. "Now the Knight needs to stop the King, destroy the spell, and clean up the mess he inadvertently made. But no one wants to help him because the King has dragons and, well. Dragons. He's not going to give up, though. He is going to correct his horrible mistake."

Minni paused as Ryan shuffled more of the paperwork, putting folders on top of stacks of folders. She honestly forgot he was still looking through them, as caught up in the story as she was. It only now occured to her that while her and her siblings may have used it to distract their mother, it was quite possible their mom had used it to distract them, from time to time.

"The Knight might be a Masterson," Minni continued once Ryan had settled in again, "but he was born without magic. Probably should have mentioned that earlier."

"Eh, you're doing fine," Ryan assured her.

"Anyway, he knows enough about magic to know the spell is tied to an amulet that the King wears. He removes that, destroys it, and the dragons go free. It's the getting to the amulet that is the problem." Minni took a breath and thought about the next part of the story. "The Knight dresses as a servant and sneaks into the castle which is guarded by dragons with orders to kill the Knight on sight. So he's very careful not to reveal his face until he gets inside. You see, none of the dragons can go inside the castle because they are all too big. Well, all but one."

"Midi," Ryan said, the name sounding ominous.

"Yeah, and… and no one can quite agree on what happens next." Minni had her own ideas, but she wasn't going to pass them off as fact when literally no one could agree on what happened at this point in the story. "If you ask my grandfather-- that is, my dad's dad--then Midi got around the spell by saying that the Knight wasn't a Knight, they were dressed as a servant, so he wasn't a Knight and therefore had no orders to kill him on sight."

Ryan crinkled his brow. "I can think of about a dozen reasons why that doesn't work, just off the top of my head. I mean, we might not know what his name was now, but the King would have. I'm sure he would have used it. You know, 'if Bob comes anywhere near this castle, kill him until he is dead,' or, whatever."

"One would think, yeah," Minni agreed. "But the other option is that the Knight did fight Midi, and either incapacitated her, or even killed her."

"Shit…"

"Yeah." Minni took a second to let that work its way through. "The Knight was trying to not only save the dragons, but stop the attacks on all the innocent people in the other kingdoms. The King was indiscriminate in his attacks."

"Still…" Ryan shook his head and put away a set of files, reaching for another. "I'm going to believe he just knocked Midi out cold."

"That's probably what happened," she said to make him feel better about it. Her mother would do the same, but Minni could tell that she didn't believe it. There is no such thing as a good man, and the Knight did what he had to do. "And so the Knight gets to the King, gets the amulet and breaks it, thereby ending the spell. He also grabs the Book of Gaerwen on his way out."

"Wait, where are the King's other Knights and guards?"

"Realizing that the castle is surrounded by several really pissed off dragons who are now free to do as they please."

Ryan blinked. "Yeah, sucks to be them."

Minni chuckled. It helped to get through the end of the story. "Well, the Knight destroys the book so it could never be used against them again. Then the dragons, after they've had their revenge, destroy the castle and fly back to wherever they came from. This includes Vask who goes back to the quarry town."

"With Midi," Ryan added.

"Right." Minni attempted a smile for him. "They settle into an abandoned quarry because it will take at least a year, some say up to five or even ten years for Vask to be able to take human form again. The Knight follows and sets up a little camp for himself in the quarry. And that's where he lives, hanging up his sword."

"Oh, that's what you mean by he waited for her." Ryan had the sudden realization. "The Knight waited until Vask was human again so they could be together. Nice."

Or he awaited a punishment that came either swiftly or agonizingly slow. A penance for what he had to do to stop the King. "So yeah, that's the story of Copper Knight."

"That's a good story." Ryan smiled, then dropped his brow. "But why is he called the Copper Knight? Wouldn't copper make terrible armor? Unless maybe it was only electroplated with copper. Wait, no, this is Dark Ages. I was reading something in one of Phil's books… um, oh, yeah, mercury gilding. You can use mercury to plate stuff with silver or gold. I wonder if works with copper?"

Minni's face had gone completely blank. It was clear she wasn't listening to him.

This did not go unnoticed by Ryan. "Um, are you okay?"

"Why, in all my years, have I never thought to fucking ask why he's called the Copper Knight?"

ELEVEN[11]

Wednesday, January 31st, 2018
12:32am

"You're in no position to ask about our family financials." Gerald was not happy, but he took the threat of me zapping them into oblivion seriously enough. "But I suppose it's no secret that it all goes to Robert, their father."

"And Aunt Lori?"

"We won't see any of her wealth," Clara informed me. "Personal items, family heirlooms, and some cash will go to her immediately family members, but all her holdings will go to whoever becomes the next pack mother of the sub-pack."

"Would that be anyone immediately related to you?" I asked while simultaneously wondering how I happened to find myself playing Miss Marple. I really needed a flowery hat for this.

"Oh, no." Clara shook her head, then looked to Gerald. "That would probably be Susanna."

"She was being groomed for it, yes," the man agreed.

Man, there are so many people in this family. I have no idea how I kept them all straight.

"Okay, well." I started going through everything I knew about Walter Blakesley, wondering why I was taking the lead on this. I'm not exactly a trained detective—not exactly a trained adult either if we're splitting hairs—and I'm only really good at one thing. Being the responsible one and solving a murder isn't anywhere close to that zone.

I guess I was doing it for Phil. He looked so damn lost right now.

Ugh, *family*.

I then remembered something. "Uncle James said Walter only wanted the *Le Bosquet d'Argus*. What is that, a painting?"

"No, it's a dairy farm, north of here," Clara said. "It's been abandoned for years."

"Why?" asked Phil.

"Something about ground water contamination?" Luke shakily answered.

"There's said to be mercury in the wells." Gerald was more confident in his answer. "There was some illegal waste dumping back in the 80s. It leaked mercury from batteries or something into the ground water. Thankfully, because where *Le Bosquet* sits and the way the watershed formed, the damage was contained."

Clara walked over to the coffee table and pulled a paper from a stack of books and files. She handed me a scanned copy of a property map which showed *Le Bosquet d'Argus* and a few other locations that were of importance to the Blakesleys. "A bunch of dairy cows died. So they shut the whole place down and moved on."

"Which explains why no one argued about Walter wanting *Le Bosquet*," I stated the obvious. "But why did he want it?"

"He didn't say," Luke answered. "I guess we all assumed he was going to try to clean it up and then do something with it, maybe turn it into housing."

"It would take a lot of effort and a lot of years," Gerald pointed out. "But he could have turned a profit on it, eventually."

"So who gets the property now?" I asked.

The Blakesleys all looked at each other, then shrugged.

"Whoever wants it, I guess," Clara said.

"Would it be worth a lot to sell?"

"No," Gerald replied bluntly. "It can be sold, just not at a price worth killing over."

I made a little herm sound and handed the map back to Clara. Money was money, if someone needed it bad enough. People get killed for seemingly small sums all the time. But then the killer would have to have a buyer ready to go. And since no one else had expressed a desire for the property, that line of reasoning seemed like a bust, until Ryan thought it through.

"What if it's not about the land?" Ryan asked the room.

"What do you mean?" I asked him back.

"It's a dairy farm, right? Which means there's buildings, equipment, that kind of thing."

"Old ones," Luke pointed out. "There's been no upkeep, so they've probably degraded into structural hazards by now."

"Maybe." Ryan shrugged and curled up into the chair he had taken by the fireplace. "But just because the ground is worthless doesn't mean you can automatically discount what's sitting on it."

"We should go check it out," Phil immediately said.

"It's like, almost one a.m.," I said.

"I don't really think any of us are planning on sleeping any time soon." Phil was starting to draw on his wizard-grade stubbornness. "This is the only lead we've had to a motive other than whatever bull theory Longtree used to intimidate Henry into confessing."

I kind of wanted to defend Longtree here. He seemed like an okay cop who was doing his job. Sure, he wasn't particularly personable, but he seemed reasonable. He could have locked up Phil the moment he found out Walter was dead, but didn't.

"I think I'd be interested as well," Gerald not-so-helpfully said. "I want my Uncle's murderer found. And I want there to be no doubt at trial as to who they are or why they did it."

"Then let's go." Phil started to move towards the door.

"Now, hold on there a minute," I said far louder than I meant, my Nebraskan accent coming out a bit thick. I coughed as everyone stared at me, then continued my thought. "Phil, the uni Longtree put on you is gonna follow you. And unless I read that map wrong, *Le Bosquet* is a bit of a way's out. It's possible they might think you're doing a runner."

Phil couldn't argue with me on that one. "Okay, so what do you suggest?"

"I'll go with Gerald here and scope it out." I always agree to do things without thinking it through, but you know, it's worked for me so far. "I'll report back with what I find. I'll even take pictures."

"Okay," Phil reluctantly agreed.

"We'll take my truck," Gerald said, heading to the door.

"I'll come with you." Luke followed after.

I turned to Ryan. "You want to come?"

He barely contained a snort. "Yeah, no, I'm going to stay here where it's warm."

Can't say I blamed him too much. "Alright, I'll see you guys in a bit."

I followed Gerald and his crew outside. We had to walk farther down the road to get to his truck. By this time, more police and police-adjacent vehicles lined the street. I suppose it could have been a coincidence that Lori Blakesley overdosed the same night Walter was murdered. If she was as upset as Clara said she had been, then mistakes could have been made.

Yeah, I didn't really believe that either.

Okay, so Gerald's truck was a newer model, but only single cab. He gestured to the back, saying, "Hop on in."

I guess he thought he was being aggressive or dominating or... something, I don't know. It was clear he wasn't expecting me to be able to one sprint-step into the truck bed and make myself comfy in the best spot. Hey, my dad has an old GMC and I had six siblings. We may or may not have attempted to throw each other out of the back of said moving vehicle at various points in time.

Attempted.

Not for a lack of trying.

Anyway, Luke, Declan, and one other joined me in the back. Gerald got into the cab with two of his minions and he wasted no time in racing down the street. Cold air blasted my face and I built up my thermal barrier out of instinct. I was too busy enjoying the view.

Old houses covered in a dusting of snow passed by like some kind of Hallmark movie set piece. Then the town gave way to an eerie two-lane road missing the center line. Tall pines and birch trees encroached on the edges, hanging low branches over the wet payment. They swayed as the truck passed underneath, dropping snow, leaves, and sticks.

The canopy would break, revealing the moon, large and bright, chasing away the darkness and deepening the shadows. I mused out loud, "So that's a Super Blue Blood Moon…"

"Technically it's only a Super Blue Moon at the moment," Declan corrected me.

"Really?" I asked, not taking my eyes off the sky.

"It's a Super Moon because the moon is full while also at its closest approach to Earth," Declan explained for me, his voice raised above the wind. "It's 'blue' because it's the second full moon in the same month. Typically there's only one."

I probably should have known all this. I'm pretty sure lunar cycles did come up in my magic schooling. Magic is just advanced physics, really, and so the gravitation pull of the moon can be very important to certain spells. I'll be damned if I can remember which. The only thing I can really remember is that the moon is moving away from the Earth, but like, hella slowly.

I looked at Declan. "So where does the blood come in?"

"That would be the eclipse," Luke answered for him. "The moon gains a tinge of red during a lunar eclipse, hence Blood Moon. But that won't occur for a few more hours."

"Huh." I learn something new every day. I just hope I remember it this time.

The pavement gave way to dirt and Gerald slowed down as the truck navigated the soft ruts. He came to a stop and killed the engine and the headlights. The only illumination came from the Super Blue Moon above. This didn't bother the men as they leapt out of the truck bed, hopping out like dogs pouncing on prey. I was about to do the same, but Declan offered his hand like a gentleman, letting me get down in a way that isn't hard on the knees.

"Watch your step," he told me and then headed towards the front of the truck with the rest of his crew and Luke.

I followed, taking in the sight of the very eerie looking farmhouse and barn. The house was one of those long rectangle types, the whole front lined by a porch with second floor windows overlooking. Chimneys stood at both ends, missing a few bricks here and there. Cold wind whistled through broken glass and years of ivy growth had completely taken over one side. The wood looked so old and decayed that I'm pretty sure it was just the leaves and termites that kept it together.

The others moved forward and I was tempted to steal Gerald's truck, getting the hell out of there before I ended up being dragged to hell. Then I remembered that I don't know how to hotwire a truck. But also, they were all werewolves and I'm a witch. Pretty sure we could collectively beat the ever-loving shit out of whatever lurks in old farmhouses. Jason, maybe?

"Let's check out the house first," Gerald said and walked up the porch steps. They creaked something awful under his feet.

"So, no flashlights?" I asked as he tugged at the door.

The cold, wet wood had become swollen shut. Gerald gave it a good push with his shoulder. Something cracked, and the door swung open. He then looked back at me, his eyes glowing like a wolf's. "Use your phone if you must."

"Not all of us have handy glow-in–the-dark eyes."

Gerald dismissed me and headed inside.

"It's an extra light reflecting piece," Declan explained as we held back. "It's called a tapetum lucidum."

Yes, I knew this. Okay, I didn't remember the name of it, but I understood the mechanics. But Declan seemed nice, so I held off on the sarcasm department. "So you retain things like that when you are human? Seems pretty handy."

"It can be, yeah."

"You coming, little witch?" Gerald shouted.

"Just making sure the crazed axe-wielding maniac gets to you first," I replied cheerfully, much to Declan's pleasure.

Pumping electricity into my bracelet—you know, just in case—I headed into the farmhouse. All I could see was five sets of glowing eyes. I nearly tased them all before I tapped down on my fight response. It was so pitch dark in there, it was ridiculous.

"Yeah, I'm not doing this." I wasn't going to use my phone because it would do that thing where everything is suddenly in silhouette, every shadow becoming long, dark, and menacing.

Instead, I summoned a ball of light. The spell is simple: you create a spherical area where you readjust the wavelength of the electromagnetic radiation in said sphere to the point it emits visible light. I mean, that's technically what happens. But seeing as wizards didn't know shit about wavelengths and photons back in the day, it was more of a 'use magic to shake that piece of air and see what happens.'

Many mistakes were made.

Once I had my sphere, I wrapped another layer of magic around it which would scatter the light when it passed through, diffusing it. I tossed it up so it would stick to the ceiling, illuminating the area in a nice soft glow. No scary shadows, but I was still standing in a set piece for some *Blair Witch* homage.

The farmhouse was old, built originally in 1818, but it looked to have been renovated a few times. And by renovated, I mean, they added some wallpaper in maybe the twenties. Did they have wallpaper in the twenties? I don't know. It was that damask design I've seen in a lot of art deco stuff. It was also peeling off the wall and molded over in places.

There were a few rooms, each wall holding up the floor above, or what was left of it. I stuck a light in all of them, what good it did. Random pieces of wood laid around, probably originally belonging to some furniture. There was also junk, like beer cans, kicked into the corners. One room had demonic-adjacent symbols drawn in spray paint. Someone had been watching too many episodes of *Supernatural*.

"None of this makes any sense." I nearly laughed. "It's like they're trying to summon a celestial water spirit in the middle of a forest with the equivalent of a string and tin can."

Gerald leaned against the door frame. "Getting a little high and mighty there?"

"Hey, if you're gonna witch, then witch right," I grumbled. Though, admittedly, it was good they didn't actually summon anything. Playing around with magic is the same as playing with chemicals in a chem lab. Everyone is having fun until they really aren't.

"This is a bust." Gerald sighed and stood.

"Yeah, I'm not seeing anything worth killing over." Even reaching out for magic, I sensed nothing.

"Let's check the barn." Gerald moved, and I followed suit.

I let the light spheres fall apart, the wavelengths going back to their usually scheduled programing. The house went dark again and I had to readjust my eyes for a moment when I went outside. The moon might have been high and bright, but there was no getting around the fact it was night.

The barn was a typical long-red type, but it's questionable if it was ever red. Any paint had long since chipped away, leaving dark hardwood that was probably some home décor tv host's wet dream of reclaimed wood. I wondered idly if that might have had something to do with Walter wanting the place. But while it might be worth making some money on the side for Walter, I doubted that would be the real reason for wanting the place. There had to be something else.

The door to the barn was on a rusted slider. It took three of them to pull it sideways enough that someone might be able to walk through. Not that this helped at all.

"It's collapsed," I said as I stuck my head through the opening, sending a light to illuminate the best it could. The ceiling timbers had fallen, taking all the roof slats with it. Years of leaves, dust, and whatever else was piled up into an impassable barrier.

Gerald, being much taller than I, peeked in over my head. "We'll have to come back tomorrow in the daylight, with tools and machinery possibly."

"I'm beginning to think this was a stupid idea." I sighed and got out of Gerald's way. "Unless there is an untapped gold mine or oil or something under this land, there is nothing above it worth killing over."

Okay, that actually gave me an idea.

I left Gerald and his men to discuss what to do about the barn and headed farther out into the grazing field. The area had been a natural clearing when the farm was built. And since it was so far from the warmth of the city, the normally tall grass was weighed down by thick layers of snow. It crunched under my feet and the freshness of it nearly made me lightheaded. I stopped in the middle of the open field and stared up at the super blue moon.

You could have told me I'd been dropped into the fairy world again, and I wouldn't argue.

I squatted down, trying not to get my jeans wet, and pressed my hand to the ground. The cold stung and I sent out a small wave of heat, along with a wide swath of magic. I had done something similar a few months before, in Montana of all places. There, I had looked for magic and instead found a magic void. Here, I tried to find anything that presented a specific range of electrical resistance.

Gold is a really good conductor. I speak from experience.

"Ma'am," Declan said, he was probably thirty feet away.

"Just prospecting for gold," I told him as I adjusted my current to search for other metals and minerals. "Or silver, or, I dunno, what's mined around here?"

"Not that, ma'am. Please, don't be alarmed."

I glanced up to see over a dozen glowing eyes staring at me. I hitched my breath as large timber wolves started to make their way from the edges of the woods. They stalked slowly through the snow, one after another emerging from the darkness until they numbered a legion.

"They know you're with us," Declan assured me.

Cold air brushed past as I stayed completely still, the crunching sound of snow, leaves, and sticks echoing in the open space. Like a rock in a river, they parted around me, heading towards the abandoned barn. The leader of the pack stopped, halting the rest. I found myself surrounded by werewolves who kept sniffing in my direction, though none bared their teeth.

"I have solemn news," Gerald voice took on a far more respectful tone than I had heard him speak before. "Walter is dead. Murdered. Stabbed with a silver knife." A grumble rolled through the ranks. "I have far worse news," Gerald continued. "Our beloved pack mother, Lori... she has also passed, poisoned by her own medication."

Silence descended on *Le Bosquet d'Argus*, as each wolf sat down, their legs buckling under the weight of their disbelief. The air itself was sucked out of the grove as they deeply inhaled, raising their heads to the sky. Mournful howls pierced the night, aimed at the moon, as if it was somehow to be blamed.

I slapped my hands over my ears, the sheer pressure of the sound stabbing at my equilibrium. I fell into the snow, curled upon myself as the werewolves rained down sadness with their cries.

TWELVE[12]

December 21st, 2013

It hit her like a bag of nostalgia falling from the height of misremembered truths, and it stank like horseshit.

"Minni!" Her younger sister flung her arms around her.

"Yeah, it's me," Minni kept them both from tipping over into the dirt, or back into the Shadow Gate.

It wasn't like Minni hadn't spent time away from Cozad, Nebraska before. She spent four years going back and forth between there and West Lafayette as she got her degree. But today, finally being able to visit home, even if only for a short time, before she had to return to her starless prison…

It really did stink like horseshit.

"Oh god, that smell." Minni covered her nose to block the unique aroma of the countryside. "How did I forget that smell?"

Her lament was completely ignored as her mother pulled her sister away so that she could be the one to hug her. "I am so glad you're home."

"Me too," she whispered back.

"Come on." Her mom started to drag her along. "Let's get indoors, get you warmed up."

It would be pointless to remind her mother that she could easily create a heat buffer and thereby avoid the cold. The woman would still tell her to wear another coat, add at least three more layers… and earmuffs. All of that with barely a dusting of snow on the ground.

Minni tried to reach for her bag but her sister had already grabbed it. It was just the two of them who met her at the Shadow Gate, something Minni was glad for. She really didn't want any kind of big production to be made. She wanted to pretend that this was just a normal visit and not a furlough for good behavior.

"It's just so good to have you home," her mother said, repeating herself.

"Good to be home." Minni played along, tampering down on the urge to comment about the situation. About how the last time she was here she was waiting for her sentence to be carried out. About how she was only alive by the grace of the council who would rather keep her around as a weapon: break glass if needed. About how everyone kept their head down, not bringing attention to their paroled daughter and sister.

Not that Minni had any doubt that her family would be by her side if push came to shove… but no one wanted to be the one to push or shove.

"There is so much to do," her mother said as they entered the kitchen of their farmhouse. "Your father is out running some errands, and your brother is upstairs. You should go tell him you're here." She may have not said it directly, but she made it obvious by the look she gave Minni. Clear the air between her and her brother, or she'd do it for them.

"I probably should go do that." Minni took her bag from her sister who got the hint. Minni didn't want her to follow her upstairs to her room. There would be time to sit and chat and all that later. Right now, the elephant in the room needed to be shot, its carcass dragged through town to the butcher shop.

Tossing her bag on the bed, Minni's old room was little more than a guest room now. Most of the rooms were. Being the fourth of seven kids, and at twenty-two, she already had in-laws and one niece, with another on the way. The Masterson's clan was a tight knit group that liked to keep space between them.

But there was one sibling still living in the house who may possibly never leave. Not that he really had a choice in the matter.

Minni walked down the hallway and knocked on a door. Silence answered her back, but she knew he was inside. She'd wait all night for him to answer, she could be stubborn like that. Stubborn enough to spend months avoiding this very discussion. But there was no putting it off anymore, and she just wanted to get it done and over with.

"I don't want to do this either," she spoke loudly enough to be heard through the door. "But we need to get this out of the way or we're just going to hurt Mom."

Ten seconds passed. Minni counted them in her head. The door swung lazily open, the room's owner not bothering to greet her or invite her in. He walked back to his desk, a slight limp to his gait. Sitting down, nearly sinking into the chair, he looked up at his sister with the only eye he had left.

"Say whatever it was you came to say," David told her, his voice far too old for someone just now sixteen.

When Minni pulled the aura, the life force, from the man in the field to keep her brother alive, that's literally all it did. It didn't magically heal him, just kept his light from burning out. The man had beaten David with a baseball bat. Broke a kneecap, some ribs, and other random bones with names Minni couldn't pronounce very well. But the killing blow—what should have been the killing blow—was the strike to the left side of his head. The skull fractured, his eye becoming damaged beyond repair.

By a miracle there was no brain damage; well, nothing that was noticeable at least. The healers said they'd want to keep an eye on him for years to come, as he was still technically growing. But the deformity of the skull was insidious in its subtly, in that you didn't know what was wrong, only that something was. The far more obvious sign of his attack was the way his left brow drooped, the bone there broken, out of place, and whatever was left of his eye now useless.

This was the first time Minni had seen her brother, face to face, since the incident. He had been with the healers for months after the attack. Minni was already back to her last semester of college when he was finally able to come home. He found excuses to avoid her on those few days she was home before being shipped off to serve out her sentence. And everything between them was left to fester.

"I'm not going to apologize," Minni told David.

"I'd honestly be surprised if you did." He chuckled tiredly. "You don't want to believe you did anything wrong."

"You were going to die." Minni bit back on her anger. "I wasn't going to let that happen."

"It wasn't your decision to make!" He held back nothing.

"It kinda was," she nearly shouted. "You were dying. I could save you, and I did."

His voice went even, cold. "What you did… was go against *everything* I stand for as a necromancer."

"Raise the dead, that's your shtick, right?" Anger was clouded Minni's judgment, her words coming out flippant and challenging.

David stood from the desk, the air in the room growing cold and dense, and it wasn't from magic. "Death is a balance. It's the culmination of life. You respect it! You don't go around ripping a person's life out of their body because you *think* you know better!"

"A life for a life, I know the deal!" The air crackled with electricity and that had everything to do with Minni. "It was you or him, and you deserved to live far more than he did!"

"You can't possibly know that," David replied with icy calm. "You don't even know his name."

That sliced into Minni, but she ignored the pain. "I don't want to know it."

"Whatever you have to do to sleep at night, sis." David nearly sneered, sinking back into his chair.

"Sleeping is easy," she said quietly. "Dreaming is hard."

Minni glanced around the room, trying to find her footing again. She saved her brother's life, she did the right thing, end of story. But it wasn't her story to write.

Necromancers had gotten a bit of a reputation as the creepy goth emo types who are probably evil. In fairness, Minni had met several who had fit that physical description, but all save one had been the nicest of people. David though, he was a picture perfect normal kid, if such a thing really existed. That is to say, there is no uniform for necromancers, nothing but the shared veneration for life.

To give the dead back their voice.

"I gave you back your life," Minni pointed out quietly.

"No, you gave me his." David glanced up at her with sadness. "What was his last meal?"

"Pumpkin pie." Minni swallowed hard, trying to choke down the taste that snuck its way up her throat. "He was going to order pecan but…"

"The diner always has pumpkin."

"Even if it's out of season."

"And it was his favorite," David was miles away when he said those words.

Magic doesn't always come with a price, but when it does, there is no price ledger. You get what it takes. Minni used her body as a conduit to transfer the man's life force. For that, the aftertaste of pumpkin pie sat heavy in her throat for months. A reminder of what she had did, what she had taken away. And although it had faded in time, it returned in that moment. She felt like vomiting.

"It's worse for me, you know…" David told her.

"But you're alive," she said, perhaps more to herself.

"And that's the only thing that matters?" His question seemed to be honest.

Something scratched at Minni's psyche, an instinct being born, or perhaps rediscovered. "I will do whatever it takes to keep the people I love safe. And I'm never going to apologize."

"And I'm never going to forgive you," he replied tiredly.

Silence stretched out between them. They knew where each other stood. The only thing to do now was move forward to wherever that might be.

Minni cleared her throat. "But we're both totally agreed we're not telling mom."

"Oh, hells no are we telling her. As far as she's concerned, we made up." David's eye went wide as if he was considering what would happen if they had to face their mother's wrath.

"We can be nice to each other for a few days," Minni said, then added, "but, you know, not too nice."

"Yeah, she'd get totally suspicious."

And on that the siblings could at least agree.

THIRTEEN[13]

Wednesday, January 31st, 2018
1:01am

"You going to be okay?" Declan asked, offering me a hand.

I was cold, wet, and miserable, but I accepted his hand anyway. "Yeah, I'm fine."

"Find anything down there?" He helped me stand.

"Nah, no buried treasure, natural or otherwise."

The howling had stopped, some of the wolves heading back out into the wood for whatever reason.

"We're heading back," Gerald called out to us. "There isn't anything here, at least nothing that can be seen in the moonlight."

I couldn't decide if this was a good or bad thing. I mean, we were no closer to figuring out who killed Walt. But also, that was kind of Longtree's job and we could have really screwed up the investigation. But we were being active, and that kept both Phil and Gerald occupied and not trying to tear someone's throat out. Metaphorically and literally.

I sent thermal heat through my clothing, especially my shoes. Steam wafted off me as I walked to the truck through the snow-covered field. The men looked at me as if I was some kind of forest witch haunting them in the night.

I mean, I am a witch, and it was night, in a forest, so...

One of the men opened the tailgate, two of the wolves jumping up into the bed. I climbed in and flopped myself down in the corner, still keeping that buffer of warm air around me. The wolves, who had been kind of doing that walking around in circles thing they do, came up to me wanting my attention.

"You're warm," Declan said as he took his own seat.

"Huh?" I frowned, it took a solid six seconds before I realized what was happening. "They have fur coats!"

"They've also been out in the snowy forest for hours," Declan pointed out, then shrugged. "You can tell them to eff-off. They understand English."

I thought it over for as much time as it took for the tailgate to be closed and Gerald to start up the engine.

"Alright, fine, but no funny business," I said as I opened my arms. I'm clearly a sucker for pouty-puppy eyes. "Keep your paws and snouts to yourselves."

The wolves quickly moved forward, curling themselves up around both sides of me so they could benefit from the heat buffer. They rested their chins on my outstretched legs, close to my knees. Not knowing where to put my hands, I gently laid them down on their backs like I would an actual dog. I glanced up at Declan and he gave me a nod.

Gerald took off back the way we came. The moon was shadowed by passing clouds, but it was still large and bright. It made for a haunting yet beautiful ride through the countryside.

My two travel companions stayed put, curling up and enjoying the heat. Their fur was soft and thick, and I started to pet them out of habit. One even offered the back of their head so I could scratch behind their ear. When I remembered that these were people, just in their wolf form, I stopped and gave Declan a panicked look.

He chuckled lightly at me. "Nothing to feel weird about. A good ear scratch is like a hug."

"Oh, okay." I breathed a sigh of relief.

By the time we got to the house, both wolves had gotten me to give them ear scratches. But as soon as we stopped on the street--about two houses down from Clara's--they were up and out of the truck. They bounded over the edge and took off in different directions. One of them headed around to the back of the house.

"I swear to god," I told Declan as we climbed out of the truck, "if you lied to me and ear scratching is some kind of foreplay, I won't murder you, but you will have *so many* regrets."

He gave me the blankest of looks. "I believe you."

"You should," I replied and got out of the way of Luke climbing over the tailgate.

"The cops are still at Aunt Lori's." Luke pointed to the police cars and coroner van sitting out front of the house.

"Yeah." I frowned. What I also noticed was that Longtree's car was absent. "We should find Phil."

I did leave Ryan to watch Phil, to keep him out of trouble. It was a good plan, up until it wasn't. And I hoped that hadn't been the case.

Declan went with Gerald who walked into the house the first wolf disappeared behind. Luke led us down the sidewalk to Clara's house. I keep calling it Clara's house but as I think I mentioned earlier, she lives there with her brother and father. It's apparently common for generations of pack members to stay together. It's like Phil said: lone wolves die early, miserable and alone.

When we got inside the house, I was very much relieved to see Phil sitting on the sofa. He looked almost like a caged animal. He perked up, but immediately frowned when he saw my look of 'don't know what to tell you, man.'

Ryan still sat close to the fireplace, reading a book he must have borrowed off the shelf. He glanced up at me and said. "Are we sure this Phil isn't a changeling?"

"Changelings don't actually exist." The 'you should know better' went without saying.

"Shapeshifter then?"

"That's more likely, yes."

"Guys!" Phil wasn't happy with us and I'm okay with that.

I pointed squarely at him. "Hey, this is what you get when you put us in charge."

Clara walked into the room with the second wolf from the truck. I think he said something to both Clara and Luke, just by the way he kind of tilted his head and the two of them responded with a nod. The wolf then took off up the stairs.

"So, you didn't find anything at the farmhouse?" Phil asked for confirmation.

"Just the set piece for the next *Cabin in the Woods*," I said and made my way over to the fire. I could feel Phil and Ryan were building up some magic static, so I wanted to siphon it off. I dropped my thermal buffer as I did so in order to make sure I wasn't reading my energy levels wrong.

"There must be another motive," Luke said but offered no suggestions.

There was a thud of feet on the stairs, an older gentleman bounding down the steps. He wasn't wearing any shoes and was pulling a sweater down over a button up shirt.

"This is our father, Robert," Clara offered. "Dad, you know Phil, Henry's brother. These are his friends, Ryan and Minni."

"We've met." Robert nodded at me, not skeevy like, just an acknowledgement that yes, we had met each other. That's when it clicked that he was the wolf, now returned to his human form. I know, I should have figured that out when he came down the stairs.

"Hey," I said slightly awkwardly.

Robert's attention was already on Phil. "Despite Walter's protests, I know your brother is a good man and would never have done this."

"Thank you." Phil seemed appreciative of the support.

"I am in agreement that we should allow the detective to do his job." Robert moved to one of the side tables and picked up a wallet and phone. "Not only do we not want to risk the case, but we have the pack to consider. We can't let this upset the families."

"The farm was a bust," Luke told him. "I think Phil can agree that we're out of options other than to trust the system."

I got good vibes from Longtree, but trusting the system as a whole? Yeah, that's too much of a stretch. Although, they were a rich white suburban family, so they definitely had the advantage here. I refrained commenting on this and instead just side-eyed Ryan, who agreed with my observation via a suitable eye-roll.

"I'm going to the station," Robert told us. "I'll let you know what I find out."

"Dad," Clara called out. "Shoes."

The man looked down at his bare toes. "Right."

After a quick run back upstairs, Robert left to go talk to Longtree. As Robert was in direct line for Jeremiah and Walter's fortunes, I'm sure Longtree would have questions of his own.

I sent a text to Uncle James. *"How's it looking?"*

"Henry is clearly covering for someone," Uncle James replied. *"My best guess would be Clara."*

I glanced over at Clara who paced slightly. Her brother sat in one of the chairs, gazing blankly into the void. Phil stared at the floor, eyes darting around as if he was thinking. Ryan was still reading by the fireplace.

"Why did you tell me that?" I sent back to Uncle James. *"Now I'm completely paranoid that I'm sitting here in a room with a murderer."*

"Yes," was his return.

Uncle James is totally not my favorite uncle.

I got another text. *"Clara wasn't with Henry between the time Walt died and Longtree interviewed him. So something Longtree said, or something Henry saw, led him to believe Clara killed Walt."*

"And you expect me to figure out what that was... how? [thinking emoji] [blank faced emoji]"

"You're a Masterson. You'll think of something."

I think Uncle James puts too much faith in our bloodline. I mean, I'm all for family pride, but we can't even prove that First Master actually existed. I know Gaerwen did, and likely so did the Copper Knight. They were both descendants of the same ancestor. But let's be real. First Master could have been an awesome wizard, or he could have been some random dude who had a lot of kids.

Sorry, it's just all this talk about family and stuff. They always make things more complicated, for better and worse. Right now the Blakesleys seemed firmly in the worse category. It wasn't really my place to try to make things better, but lately I've been wondering if my place is wherever I am standing.

"Bathroom?" I asked to whomever would answer.

"There's a guest one down the hall," Clara pointed in the general direction. "Third door on the left."

"Thanks." I easily found the little half-bath that may have been built into a former closet of some sort. It amazed me how these werewolves could live in a house with so many walls and small spaces.

On the way back, I let myself peek into the rooms on the bottom floor. The kitchen with a connected dining room took up a good third of it. But I hit the jackpot with what looked like a common computer room slash study.

There were three desks, each occupied by different people: Clara, Luke, and their father. Family photos where hung up on the wall, the ones with their mother very prominent. I guess they didn't believe that she ran away on them—or maybe it was just wishful thinking. There was also a few pictures of them in their wolf form as both pups and then adults. They had the same coloring as their human hair, looking almost like border collie, but large and with sharp teeth. They seemed to have gotten the coloring from their mother.

As interesting as that all was, it wasn't what I was there for. I started to rummage through the paperwork and stuff sitting on the desks. I had no idea if anything of importance would be there. Or what something of importance would even look like. Pretty sure it wasn't USGS maps or Chinese take-out menus.

Then I realized I was being fucking ridiculous.

I'm not a detective. Hell, I'm barely a witch.

"What are you doing?" Clara asked from the door.

Busted.

Okay, Minni, stay cool, you got this. Just play it off. Play the dopey Midwesterner. No one has to know you were looking for evidence in a murder investigation and you suspected Clara of being the murderer.

"Did you kill Walter?" I asked her.

Or, you know, I could do that.

"What?" Clara blinked, looking at me as if I asked her if the moon was made of cheese. "No... what?"

I had no idea if she was guilty or not. She certainly looked confused by the question.

"We know Henry confessed," I told her, driving that train right off the cliff. "So he either thought you or Phil murdered Walter. Since Phil has an alibi, I'm guessing he thinks it was you."

Clara thought this over for a second, then her face went soft. "Oh, Henry."

"Do you know why Henry would suspect you?" I was willing to give her the benefit of the doubt. I looked into her eyes and didn't see anything reflected back in them. I didn't think this woman had so much as killed a rabbit, let alone one, possibly two, people. "I sincerely doubt he heard someone had been murdered and immediately thought you did it."

Clara wasn't particularly amused by that comment. She moved towards the desk, staring down at the papers. "I don't know. I truly don't."

"You're saying you don't have a motive?"

She blanched. "Of course I have a motive. Walter was trying to keep me and Henry from marrying. But that's not worth killing over. Aunt Lori would have told him to stay out of it. That's why I went to talk to her."

And not long later, Aunt Lori was dead. "Did she refuse?"

"No." Clara scoffed as if I'd asked a ridiculous question. "Aunt Lori had already given her blessing for Henry to join the pack. If she rescinded it because Uncle Walter was making a fuss, it would set a bad precedence. Lori is the older sibling, and she never let Walt forget it."

Right, well, Clara was too invested to be lying. At least, that's how it felt to me. I didn't know the woman long enough to know how well of a liar she was. I decided to drop that line of questioning for the moment. There were other avenues to consider. I gestured to the various maps and land… thingies that were strung about. "What's all this about?"

"My father is asking for Uncle Jeremiah's commercial real estate. I couldn't care less about any of those holdings." Clara picked up several USGS maps and laid them side by side, seven in total. "But he had a lot of valuable assets. He had a will, but our family lawyer said he nulled it last year. He was supposed to write up a new one and never did. That's why Mr. Masterson was called in, to help sort out the mess."

I honestly had no idea what I was looking at. I mean, I had a general idea because a map is a map, but I didn't know the context. I couldn't tell what made one piece of property more valuable than another.

"Where's *Le Bosquet*?" The map Clara had showed me earlier was a simple print out from Google Maps. It wasn't a fancy USGS map with elevations and other geological thingies.

Clara frowned and shuffled through the paperwork. "I don't know. Probably tossed. Walter was the only one who wanted the land, as damaged as it is."

"Right, the mercury," I trailed off as something finally clicked. "The mercury that doesn't exist."

"Huh?"

I closed my eyes and thought back to when I stood in the field. I had sent out an electrical current, looking for any kind of resistance, or lack thereof. I hadn't discovered any secret cache's of gold, silver, or even oil. I know that because, well, gold is a great conductor… And mercury is not too shabby, either.

"I did my own version of ground penetrating radar," I explained to her. "I found the water table and bedrock. Nothing was out of the ordinary. If there was a sizable enough amount of mercury to warrant abandoning the land, it's not there anymore."

"That's odd." She shuffled through the papers again. "I know I saw a report regarding the soil. The land is contaminated."

"I don't know what to tell you." Because I honestly didn't. I mean, I'm not exactly scientific equipment, nor do I have any studies in geology. I just know what I felt. "I suppose I could have read it wrong but, electricity is kind of my thing."

Clara was intent on finding the USGS paperwork,. She might have gotten a tad manic but I think that had more to do with her finding an outlet to her general frustrations than a need to see the report. She stopped when the doorbell rang through the house. We walked back to the living room, just as Luke was opening the door.

"Please don't be pixies," I muttered.

"What?"

"Don't worry about it."

"Hello again, Miss Masterson," the dark-haired woman said when she saw me. You would think she was being polite, but you would be wrong.

"Oh, hey, Agent Ross." I awkwardly waved at her. "Um, what are you doing here?"

"I was about to ask you and Mr. McCree the same thing."

Clara looked between us. "You know each other?"

"After a fashion," I answered. "She called me a janitor and I fought a dragon to prove her... right? Yeah, I'm pretty sure that's how that went down."

"You fought a dragon?" Clara reacted as most people do when I casually let that slip. That is, she looked at me like I was either lying or completely insane. One of these is probably true.

"I called you a janitor *after* you fought the dragon," Ross helpfully pointed out. "The first time."

"Really?" I think she was right, actually. "That whole weekend just kinda blended together."

FOURTEEN[14]

April 14th, 2014

Phil — I literally have no idea what day it is right now. Time zones are the worst. — Minni

Minni was unsure if a witch had ever sent a message via sender whilst hurling through the air at thirty-five thousand feet. Considering no witch would even attempt to fly in an airplane when there are perfectly good Shadow Gates, Minni was fairly confident that this was a first.

But then she remembered that planes didn't always have electronics, so maybe it wasn't.

A flight attendant came by and Minni closed the sender, packing it away in her carry-on. If her phone was to be trusted—Minni was highly suspicious that it was—then it was late enough in New York that Phil would be asleep anyway. So she stretched out, immensely glad that her benefactors sprung for first class, and took yet another nap.

Three weeks earlier, Minni got a message from Phil asking her to come by the shop after work. Despite his assurance that it wasn't anything major, anxiety and trepidation churned through her. The only times she ever got called to Phil's were usually for an emergency. There was some fire that Phil needed help putting out. The fact this summons was casual kicked Minni's paranoia up to an eleven.

The shop was still open, so she took that as a good sign. When she walked in, Ryan glanced up. He looked far too neutral, like he was trying to be on his best behavior.

"What's going on?" she asked him in a low voice.

"There's a guy from one of the magic councils in there," he said, gesturing to the back room. "But not a local one."

"What do you mean, not local?"

"Like, not even from this continent," he clarified. "I think he's from the Emirates."

Minni's fear of councilmen mixed with her confusion. Did anyone outside of the continental United States even know about her and what she did? Let alone one from the other side of the world? She guessed she was about to find out.

Pushing the curtain to the side, Minni walked into the back room. Three people instantly looked up at her. Phil sat in Ryan's chair, cup of tea in hand. Two others were on the sofa. The councilman was obvious, his aura bright and heavy with magic. He was a gentleman of Middle Eastern descent, wearing a long business jacket over a button up, a keffiyeh on his head with an agal keeping it in place. The woman sitting next to him might have just robbed a Saks Fifth Avenue.

"Minni," Phil said, putting down his tea and standing up. "Thanks for coming by."

She didn't bother to hide her continued confusion.

"Let me introduce Councilman Juma Saleh of the United Arab Emirates," Phil said as the man stood, nodding at her. "And this is Iris Edwards, local business owner."

"Hi," Minni replied very neutrally.

"This is Dominique Masterson," Phil introduced her.

"Can I call you Minni?" Iris asked in an accent that put her a little farther west than New York City. She was mid-fifties, with that air of consummate businesswoman. Not a stich of magic in her, so she wasn't a Forsaken either.

"Sure." The only thing keeping Minni from rabbiting was the fact Phil was there and didn't act like he was under any kind of spell. She had an escape plan ready though, if it came to that.

The councilman judged her critically. "It is said you can bleed off a wizard's excess magic so that it does not interfere with electronics."

Minni looked to Phil. Was the day she had been dreading finally coming to pass?

"They want to hire you, Minni," Phil explained, reading the trepidation on her face.

"Hire… me?" Minni was sure she didn't hear that right.

"How much do you know about international trade, Miss Masterson?" Juma asked her.

"How much do you think?" she couldn't help but respond.

Juma simply glanced over at Phil. "I see what you mean."

"It's hardly a deal-breaker," Iris tsked at both of them.

"As long as she can perform as promised."

"Hey." Minni got defensive, not liking being spoken of as a commodity. Something ticked over her in brain. All sense of self-preservation gone, she didn't care anymore that this man was a councilman.

"Minni," Phil said in his calming voice. "They want to hire you to be a magic sink."

"What?"

"Just for a week," Iris explained, moving in front of Juma, flashing her predatory professional smile. "You see, the world is ever changing and sometimes concessions have to be made. There are a few businessmen out of Dubai—magic users—who wish to make some important sales and acquisitions… but there is a slight snag."

Minni stared at her blankly, unimpressed.

The woman was completely unphased. "They wish to do business with a company, which is based in California, and ran by TechnoMages."

Juma made an annoying huff.

"The Mages are being difficult," Iris continued. "They think they can hold certain things for ransom, make the wizards come to them. As you well know, magic users don't really do well in TechoMage territory. And even if they wanted to risk going to California via Shadow Gate, we can't put it past the Mages to call the authorities on them. The wizards won't be able to pass an exanimation by immigration and customs and we all know how badly that could end up."

Immigration hated magic users because of our use of the Shadow Gates, even though the gates have rarely ever been used to do anything nefarious. They wouldn't treat the delegation well.

Minni looked past her to Juma. "And you want to do business with these people?"

"Not personally," he said with another huff. "But my kinsmen in question are wealthy and powerful. It would do no good to let them be manipulated by the TechnoMages. They need to show strength. That is where you come in."

It all pieced together for Minni. "You want me to travel with these guys, sink their magic, so they can thumb their noses directly at the TechoMages?"

"Essentially," Juma agreed. "I know that you are, for a lack of better term, on probation with an American magic council. I have come as a representative of our own council, not to overrule that sentence, but to take responsibility of you for this temporary request."

Minni clenched her jaw, wondering just how much this man knew about what she did to get herself into this situation in the first place. And just how in the hell did he know about it anyway? The answer seemed to be standing in front of her.

"I run a travel business," Iris said as if Minni had verbally asked. "I work with magic users and their unique requirements."

"You make it sound like we all have a nut allergy," Minni said wryly.

"Some do." Iris nodded sagely. "I provide transport to and from Shadow Gates and guides that can take them through low-tech areas. And I can also provide amulets that will sink their magic but we both know that making them takes a lot of effort and they typically don't last long enough to warrant it."

"And I am no assembly required." Minni sighed and then looked to Phil. "I assume our council signed off on this?"

"Yes." He nodded. "But, Minni, the council isn't requiring you to do this. You can say no."

"But if you say yes," Iris said with a bright smile, "then you'll be well compensated."

"Wait, so you literally meant hired?" Minni wasn't a hundred percent sure why she had assumed hiring her was more metaphorical rather than literal. "Like, I'll get paid?"

"Oh, yes." Iris grabbed a leather-bound notebook from the table, flipping it open. "Now, you'll be required to take a plane to Dubai, then fly to San Francisco and back with the business delegation, then return to New York. All that will be paid for, first class. You do have a passport, correct?"

Most wizards didn't get one because, well, they don't typically go through passport control when traveling via Shadow Gates. But in college, one of her friends got married in Cozumel. She was told she could just get a PASS card, but since she'd been mistaken for Mexican far too many times, she opted for the full passport *and* PASS card. "Yeah, should still be good. They last ten years, right?"

"Excellent." Iris continued. "Your room and three meals a day will be paid for. As will any entry fees, tickets to games or concerts, whatever the TechnoMages try to throw at them. You won't be expected to spend a single dime of your own money, except for any personal things you wish to buy."

Minni's head was starting to spin. "Just how long is this supposed to take?"

"A whole week in mid-July," she said as if it was nothing.

"I have a full time job, you know."

"Do you have vacation days?" Iris asked and Minni was already doing the mental math on that.

"I mean, yeah." She had a week and a half left, plus sick time. "But those are *my* days."

"Understandable," Iris said with a sagely nod. "So, I have priced up a per diem for you. Then added four times your salary for a forty-hour work week, though, I admit, I made a guess to your actual salary based on industry standards so that can be adjusted if needed. All that together comes to…"

Iris turned the notebook around so she could see the numbers. Minni got to the bottom and choked.

"And that's after taxes," Iris said, pointing to the line that took out standard state and federal. "I'll provide all the tax forms you need so Uncle Sam doesn't have a fit. Oh, and don't worry about my fees, that's a separate billing."

Minni got the distinct impression that the woman was going to make bank whether or not Minni said yes. All she could do was look at Juma and say, "These wizards are willing to fork over that kind of cash just so they can throw a middle finger to the TechnoMages?"

"Trust me," Juma said with a grave smile. "That is pocket change compared to what they'll get out of the deal by not bowing to the TechnoMages."

When it came to business, Minni didn't know a hell of a lot, it wasn't really her thing. But she did understand that when billions of dollars are on the line, thousands may as well be counted as pennies. And curse herself, she was already thinking about what she could do with the money.

Well, if the councils only kept her around because she might be useful, then she might as well be useful. And if she could get enough money out of it to get her own apartment, then why not take advantage of the situation?

Her boss signed off on her vacation even though it was a bit short notice. She said she was taking a trip to California with some friends. She neglected to mention that her friends were Dubai businessmen and she was getting to San Francisco via the United Arab Emirates.

Her stop inside the Emirates was very short. She only left the airport long enough to have a shower, eat some food, and take a short nap. Then she was flying to California with several magic users taking up most of the seats in first class. They all looked nervous, having never flown before.

Minni decided to take another nap. This, of course, scared the crap out of the businessmen who thought she'd have to be actively sinking their magic and therefore be awake. She assured them that as long as they didn't perform magic in an airplane as it flew a mile up in the sky via the aid of a shit ton of electronics... then they were okay. She would easily absorb the minimal static they produced as she slept. It was just something she did. She liked energy. It made her feel comfortable and safe.

None of them dared to cast so much as a sending spell.

Of course, she didn't mention she had to make sure she didn't start taking electrical energy from the actual plane. But magic and its related parts hum at a different frequency than electronics. It was quite easy for Minni to focus on their auras, grab ahold of them—metaphorically speaking—then tether them all together. She then became a grounding wire, or a sponge, however they wanted to look at it.

They were separated at customs when they got to the San Francisco International Airport because she had an American passport. The distance wasn't bad enough for her to lose her connection to them. She was more annoyed at the Customs agent who looked at her as if her passport must be fake. That reminded her why she never travelled like normal people... at least there are no TSA agents at the Shadow Gates.

Minni was given a hotel room in the middle of everyone else's as they took up an entire floor. Her schedule was strict, making sure she would always be where they needed her to be in order to sink their magic. She was also told she must look professional at times, so no jeans and t-shirts. She was also not allowed to sit in on the meetings themselves because of the sensitive corporate information being discussed.

On the first day she found herself sitting outside a board room, bored out of her skull. The TechnoMages would not allow her to bring her phone into the building. Minni thought this was ultimately a good idea as they could have easily hacked it and found... well, not a lot, really. But there were those photos of her twenty-first birthday party...

"Think of the money, Minni," she whispered to herself. "Think of the money."

Something poked at her, almost like a static shock, but she absorbed those without thought. This was far more sharp and concise. Minni sat up from where she was slouched in the chair and felt around with her magic. It happened again, a little firmer, against her leg. Opening her Third Eye, she looked for the lines of electrical energy that could be running through the floor or wall. The pulse happened again, sliding across the ground, following the metal bars in the flooring, then up the leg of the chair to poke her in the thigh.

Back tracing her eyes landed on a man, probably mid-twenties, sitting in a chair on the opposite wall a few feet down from her. He was dressed like a typical Silicon Valley bro: polo shirt, cargo pants, and Timberland boots. It's like they dressed what they *thought* the average person looked like. They didn't take into account the fact their wardrobe probably cost more than a month of her salary, the look co-opted by too many rich douches.

Minni sent a pulse of electricity back at him, which he apparently wasn't expecting. He jumped ever so slightly in his chair and she got a better look at him. Short dark hair, Asian features, and seriously annoyed.

"Dude," Minni called out. "If you want to know what kind of anti-TechoMage stuff I can do, you just needed to ask."

"We're not TechnoMages," the man countered quickly. "We're TechnoWizards."

"No, no you are not," Minni told him bluntly.

"Yes, we are."

"No, you're not."

"Yes. We are."

"Wizards have inherent magic." Minni huffed. "Mages, or magicians, create the allusion of magic. You're using technology to create the allusion of magic, therefore you're a magician."

"Wizards don't have inherent magic," he snarked back. "That's sorcerers. Wizards are simply people who can use magic, whether inherent or not. If you all can co-opt the wizard name because the PR's better, then so can we."

"But you aren't *using* magic." Minni might have sounded a bit more petulant than she wanted to, but he started it. "You have some piece of tech tucked up your sleeve. Just because you have precision control, doesn't make you a magic user."

Another pulse of electricity surged at her. She batted it back easily, like a return serve of a tennis match. They glared at each other, electricity beginning to bounce back and forth between them, increasing in intensity as it went.

Until the lights flickered and they both stopped, glancing up at the overhead bulbs guiltily.

Mr. Watkins, one of the TechoMage coven leaders who also happened to be the CFO of a multi-billion-dollar company, walked out of the board room. He was in his late fifties and dressed slightly more professional, wearing a button up and slacks. "What is going on?"

"He started it," Minni said, then realized that may not have been the most diplomatic thing she could have said. Sure, this wasn't official council business, but Wizard-TechnoMage relations was kind of on par with Apple and Android users. A fistfight could break out at any given moment.

Watkins gave the other man the same look she had seen Phil give her on a multiple of occasions. "Jonas, there is no need to test Miss Masterson's abilities. She's hardly the first magic sink we've run across."

Minni's eyes snapped towards him, her mouth open to ask a question. It was clear from how he sharply looked at her that he would not be answering anything, and she should just chew on that little fact for a while. Minni silently cursed him. With words, not with magic, though she was tempted.

"Yes, sir." Jonas was acceptably repentant.

"Jonas will be your shadow for the rest of your stay," Watkins told her. "At least try to get along."

Watkins didn't bother to give her a chance to answer, as snarky as it would have been, and went back into the room.

Minni glanced over at Jonas and said, "Still a magician."

It was a miracle they didn't end up starting a war.

Every chance they got to annoy each other; they took it. Whether it was strategic electric shocks, or making the other spill their food down their shirt. Nothing *seemed* to be off limits, but there was a limit. As soon as their little pissing match might bleed over and affect others, they both stopped.

There didn't seem to be any true animosity between them. One would think they were siblings who were bored while their parents hosted a dinner party.

At the end of the trip, since negotiations were successful and apparently everyone was going to make a ton of money, they had a party on a large luxury yacht anchored out in the Bay. Minni found herself sitting on the starboard side, looking out across the water, trying to do the mental math of what housing she could afford long-term with the extra cash she was making.

She just needed to figure out how to explain said extra cash to her current roommates.

Don't get her wrong, she liked them. Stacey had become one of her best friends. But Minni's whole life she had been crowded. She grew up with six siblings, then she lived in a dorm room. Everything was communal and sometimes sharing was a contact sport. She was only living in New York City because it was that or a jail cell. She wanted a place that was hers, something she didn't have to share. If that made her selfish, then fine, it wouldn't be the worst thing she's ever done. Just add it to the list.

Jonas walked up and slumped down on the bench beside her, beer in his hand. He didn't say anything, just swigged his drink as they both watched the lull of the waves.

"Do you know what we have in common?" he asked.

"We both have racial stereotypes imposed on us?"

"Well, that." Jonas took another swig of his beer, downing it as if it burned like whisky. "And we're both fuck-ups."

That was the last thing she expected to hear, and in such a serious voice. Minni turned and looked at him, about to verbally speak the word 'what,' except he stood up and started to wander off. So Minni called out, "What can be worse than murder?"

He stopped and said over his shoulder, "That's a good question."

Minni considered walking after him, finding out exactly what he was talking about. It never occurred to her that watching her would be some form of punishment. What could he have even done to deserve it? There was probably a long story there, and eventually Minni decided to let it be. Last thing she needed was to get mixed up in any TechoMage drama. In a few hours she'd be on a plane, her job nearly completed.

If they ever wanted her to do this again, she was definitely going to ask for a higher per diem.

When she touched back down in New York City, she was exhausted. Had she not been able to use her magic to give herself a quick boost, coffee might not have been enough to keep Minni awake when she got to Phil's.

Iris was there, waiting for her.

"Minni," Iris said with that broad business smile. "I have already heard mostly good things about your work." Minni snorted. "Juma and the others are very pleased with the results."

"What were the odds against me?" Minni asked Ryan who was sitting over on the sofa.

"I'll have you know I didn't bet against you," he said with a little disdain. "I covered the spread."

"That's smart."

"Minni." Iris brought the attention back to her, grabbing a manila envelope off the table and passing it over. "Your check is inside, along with all the proper tax forms you'll need."

"Great, thanks." Minni couldn't cover the thrill it gave her to know that tomorrow she would be cashing it. A week of doing nothing but following a bunch of stuffy businessmen around felt worth it now.

"You know, Minni." Iris sounded far too conspiratorial for Minni's liking. "There is money to be made here. Do you know how much a wizard might pay to be able to stand in Times Square at New Year's Eve without worry? To see a Broadway play and not have to fear literally bringing down the house?"

Minni knew exactly what Iris was saying. The usefulness of Minni's abilities were never lost on her. She used them to help out her family, her friends back in Nebraska, Phil, and other coven members. Normally it was for more important legal things, like helping them be able to give a deposition against a corrupt mortgage company without frying the video recorder. And once she went with a bunch of homeschooled young wizards to the American Museum of Natural History, as well as a few other local education venues.

But… it was always a service she did. Something to help people out. Free of charge. Except she did expect coffee and donuts if she had to sit at the DMV.

Could she really start charging for other things though?

For luxuries?

And once she started, where would it end?

"You don't have to give me your answer today, Minni," Iris said with a smile. "Just… have a think about it."

Thinking was sometimes—well often—something Minni didn't do very well.

FIFTEEN[15]

May 15th, 2014

"So, what do you think?"

"This place is huge," Stacey said, standing in the middle of the empty apartment.

"You think?" Minni was never going to get used to the relative concept of size when it came to New York City verses Nebraska.

"You can actually see a delineation between the kitchen and the living room." Stacey was in awe. "There is enough space here for a table, or a kitchen isle."

"We have that at our apartment," Minni pointed out.

"But this is a one bedroom." Stacey wandered off, going into the small hall that connected the bedroom and bathroom.

"Well, your friend likes it," said the real estate agent, Wendy, who was standing off to the side.

"Yeah, but she's not the one who's going to be paying for it, though," Minni replied dourly.

"Holy shit!" Stacey called out, sticking her head out of the bathroom. "It has a stackable!"

"Oh!" Wendy quickly raised her hand. "Those don't come with the apartment unless you want to pay a separate fee. But the hookups are there if you want to bring in your own."

"You can fit a queen-sized bed in here!" Stacey shouted from the bedroom.

Minni already liked the apartment, that wasn't in question. It was close to work. It was of a decent enough size that she didn't feel claustrophobic. She didn't have to share it with anyone. And it happened to be on 33rd street. Three's are good numbers for witches.

It was the price though.

Four very large digits a month and that didn't include bills. Okay, her electric bill would always be low but that was beside the point. She had to put down a substantial deposit and prove that her income was enough to be able to continue to afford the rent. With what she got from helping the businessmen from Dubai out, she could both afford the deposit and the first few months rent.

After that though…

If she wanted to keep it, she was going to have to take the job with Iris. She wasn't going to go on one of those big trips all the time. That was just a question of keeping her sanity intact. But if she took maybe one big job a year, and then did the tour guide thing locally. Take some wizards to go see *Wicked*. Pop through a Shadow Gate down to Orlando for a weekend so a family could visit the theme parks. At least in that situation she could actually go on the rides as well.

It just came down to an ethical quandary with her.

She'd still go with someone to the DMV if they needed to renew an ID, no charge save coffee. It would only be the luxuries she would get paid for. But then what really defined a luxury? Not every family could pay to go to Disney World, let alone pay her fee on top. But she wasn't a luxury. They had to either use her or dump a lot into anti-magic medallions and then hope they last.

And she had to be honest with herself. Would she be here, in the position to even consider taking the tour guide job, if she hadn't murdered that man in the sunflower field?

Her parents always told her to keep her ability not so much a secret, just don't advertise it. Performing a Rasputin like that was certainly the opposite of keeping a low profile. And every time she helped out Phil with a magic misstep, it was just another neon sign saying to the world that Minni Masterson is… useful.

Like a hammer, she could be a weapon or simply a tool.

One that was going to benefit from their crime.

She should have thought about that more before she took the money. But the check was cashed.

"Ah, Wendy?" Stacey walked back into the living room, seeing the pensive look on Minni's face. "Give us a second?"

"Of course." The woman smiled, knowing that Stacey was on her side. "I need to make a call anyway. But before I step out, I'll remind you that this place has already been on the market for two days. So if you don't get in now, then someone else *will* by tomorrow."

Wendy wasn't being superlative. As Minni learned while trying find a shared apartment when she first moved to New York, places went quick. This one only got an extra day reprieve because of the price tag. She wouldn't be surprised if Wendy walked back in and said, "Oops, sorry, it just got rented out." Part of her wished it would happen.

"Okay, Minni," Stacey said after Wendy left, "spill."

Minni rolled her eyes and walked over to the kitchen, trying to figure out what to say. She had already learned that if she didn't say something, Stacey would pry it out of her. The woman may not have magic, but she could have fooled Minni. "I know this is an amazing apartment. I just don't know if this is what I want to spend my money on."

"It's not every day your family sells mineral rights," Stacey said as she came to stand next to her. That had been the story Minni told to explain where the money came from. No one even questioned it. But then none of them studied geology. "And this is something that you've wanted since you first came to New York."

"True." Minni couldn't argue with that fact. She always felt like she was in a cage. She *was* in a cage if she was honest. She needed something that was hers. One more thing the council couldn't take away from her.

"And you said you had a part time job set up," Stacey continued. "Something to help with the rent?"

"It all sounds perfect." Minni sighed. "On paper."

"You don't know if it will work unless you put it into practice," she pointed out.

Minni scrunched her brow. "You really want me to rent this apartment, don't you?"

"I want you to be happy, Minni," Stacey said so seriously that it put a lump in Minni's throat. "You've never really been happy since I met you. Sure, we've had some fun times, but deep down, you just… act like you're serving out a prison sentence."

The woman had no idea how accurate she was.

Minni let out short laugh.

"I'm serious." Stacey took her by the shoulder and turned Minni to face her. "If you want to take all this money and give it to a charity, then that's fine. But using it to make yourself a home in this craptastic economy that we have doesn't make you a bad person. It makes you human."

But Minni wasn't human. She was a witch.

She had the power to bend physics to her will.

Some would say that no one should ever have such abilities and witches should be put to death. Others would say that those who have the ability to affect change should use that ability to make a better world no matter the cost. Others still would say that there is no such thing as a good person, only an evil one who understands that everyone else is as important as they are.

SIXTEEN[16]

"Agent Ross?" Phil joined us in the now crowded entryway. "What are you doing here?"

"I already asked that," I told him.

"Let's take this into the living room." Clara ushered us through to the larger area.

Once we got ourselves settled, Ross crossed her arms and did her best impression of a waiter who thought you'd leave them a bigger tip. "As I said, I'm FBI Special Agent Ross, and I work for the New York City field office. I'm tasked with making sure that magic and paranormal issues never make it into official reports."

"Then what are you doing here?" I was a bit confused, which happens a lot.

"Do you want me to start with a pack mother dying under questionable circumstances, or a werewolf being murdered with a silver dagger?" Ross has a dry snark, she's growing on me.

"Silver being the only thing that can kill a werewolf is just a myth," I told her.

"Yes, I'm aware." Ross turned her focus to the so-called adult in the room. "Mr. McCree, I understand that your brother confessed to the murder of Walter Blakesley."

"He didn't do it," Phil sounded like a kicked puppy. "I don't know why he confessed, but my brother wouldn't do this."

Ross sighed and rubbed the bridge of her nose. "Okay, then who did?"

"I… don't know, yet."

"Of course you don't." The agent had also perfected the art of the blank stare. "I would like to speak to you all individually, if that would be alright?"

"Yes, of course," Clara volunteered us. "I have some questions of my own. Why don't we head into the study?"

"That's a good idea." Ross seemed happy to take any invitation to get this over with. I had a feeling she thought this was just as much of a magical goose chase as I did.

Ross and Clara went into the study to discuss the night's events and I debated telling Phil about what Uncle James said. I asked myself... what would Phil do if it was me in his position? Then I realized that was a horrible analogy. I would have already burned down the police station and been halfway to Canada with my brother by now.

"*I don't think it was Clara,*" I texted Uncle James.

"*You don't think Clara murdered Walter or you don't think she's the one Henry is covering for?*" he replied a few minutes later.

"*She didn't kill anyone, can't be sure about the other.*"

"*That gets us nowhere closer to the truth.*" I could literally hear my uncle's monotone delivery of the line.

I responded with, "*The truth is out there.*"

"*[unamused emoji]*"

I didn't even know my uncle knew how to use emojis. After I recovered from that initial shock, I sent, "*The FBI is here. Agent Ross. Met her back in September, the whole Canton thing.*"

"*She was here earlier, talked to Longtree. I get the feeling she's going to leave the case to him and sweep whatever needs to be swept under the rug. Which might not be much.*"

"*I am pretty sure this case has nothing to do with werewolves or the supernatural.*"

"*That doesn't make the victim any less of a werewolf.*"

"Miss Masterson." Ross got my attention. I looked up to see Luke returning from his sit-down with the agent. Phil already had his turn and Ryan was curled up in a chair in front of the fire like a cat. The kid looked at a loss of what to do. Neither of us were really built for this kind of situation. But we weren't going to leave Phil alone.

"Right, coming." I tucked my phone away and followed the agent into the study.

Ross had a small notebook and pen, flipping to a new page. "Okay, tell me your version of events?"

"Phil called me to come bail him out. I did. Ran into my Uncle. Had some Dunkin'." I'm pretty proud of how I managed to condense all that. "Oh, I totally have an alibi for the murders."

"Detective Longtree did mention that, yes." Ross made a note. "Now, how well do you know Henry McCree?"

"Met him a few times, seemed like an okay guy."

Ross stared at me for a long moment. "In your experienced opinion, do you think he's capable of murder?"

I can't believe she went there. "Way to go for the jugular."

"Miss Masterson," Ross sighed and sat back in her chair. "It's late. I was dragged out of bed and I don't want to be here anymore than you do. I was ready to write all of this off as coincidence, until I saw who was involved."

"Misplace Delaware one time and you get a reputation."

"Oh, you and Mr. McCree have had one for much longer than that."

"Yeah, that's fair." What? It was.

"So, who do you think killed Walter Blakesley?" she asked.

"If I knew, I would tell you," I said honestly. Usually my paranoia kicks in around cops, or cop-adjacent individuals, but this time, I had to believe that getting the truth out there was more important. "I want Henry to be innocent and he's just covering for someone, but I'm pretty sure Clara didn't do it, and I know for a fact Phil didn't. Beyond that, your guess is probably better than mine. You're the professional."

Ross stared at me for a solid moment, thinking. "Alright."

"Alright?"

"It's clear you don't know anything substantial about this case, Miss Masterson." Ross stood from her seat.

"Man, why you gotta be so mean?" I admit, I was a little offended, even though she was right.

"I think I should approach this from another angle," she said and gestured to the door.

"What other angle?

Ross didn't answer me as she walked out of the room. I followed because, I mean, what else am I going to go do? Back in the living room, Clara and Phil discussed something as Luke stood in front of the fireplace, Ryan still in the chair.

"Mr. McCree." Ross got his attention. "I'd like you to accompany me to the scene of Walter Blakesley's murder."

"Um, sure, why?" he replied as he stood.

"I want to know if there were any magical components to the crime," she told him. "I want to rule out a few things, but being a Forsaken, I don't have the finesse required for such a task." She was basically admitting that practice makes perfect but since she doesn't practice… "I could call in another wizard, but you're already here."

"Wait." I held up my hand. "Wouldn't Phil be a conflict of interest in this?"

"Minni has a point," Phil agreed.

"One of which I am well aware," Ross replied, somewhat impatiently. "I have my reasons for being able to trust Mr. McCree in this matter."

"Such as?" I asked.

"For starters Miss Masterson, he's not you."

"Hey," Phil started to defend me.

"No." I cut him off. "That's valid."

Clara stood. "Well, if you're all going, I'm going."

"More the merrier." Ross was clearly indifferent.

"I'm going." I sighed, glancing over at Ryan. "You, too."

Ryan looked confused. "Why do I have to come?"

"Because if I suffer, we all suffer." Sarcasm is my default, but in truth, Ryan had a different, more sneaky, way of looking at things than neither Phil or I did. I had a feeling he was going to become more useful than he realized he would be.

"I'll stay here," Luke said, "in case father comes back."

Clara didn't argue with her brother and grabbed her coat. We all got rebundled and headed out. Walter's house wasn't that far, just a few lots away. Apparently the whole pack lived in the same something-square block radius. It was old-money housing, too. And it looked like things were starting to wind down at Aunt Lori's place. Most of the emergency vehicles were gone.

When we got to Walter's house, Gerald opened the door , eyeing us warily. "Agent Ross."

"I've come to take another look at the crime scene," she told him in a manner that suggested it wasn't a request.

Gerald clearly considered slamming the door in our faces, but I suppose his curiosity got the better of him.

The house was about what I expected of some old guy who came from old money. Which is to say it was every shade of brown and anything would break if you just looked at it sideways. There were also plenty of hunting trophies on the wall. It occurred to me that the elk were probably literally hunted and taken down by a werewolf in their wolf form.

Not really sure how I feel about that.

Anyway, like Clara's house, the kitchen was in the back, leading out into the yard where Walter Blakesley died. Blood still pooled in the snow muddied dirt. As was described, the killer would have had to walk past the kitchen to get a silver knife rather than taking one of the nice ceramic ones in the butcher's block. Plus, the silver knife was in a case that had to be opened, not exactly a handy reach.

Despite what Ross said, committing one murder does not an expert make, but, yeah, I would have totally gone for the easier weapon. Which, okay, let's back up a second. The easier weapon, for me, would just be a simple lightning bolt to the heart. But when I saw my brother lying there dying, I didn't want to just stop his attacker… I wanted blood and vengeance. I grabbed the baseball bat laying on the ground and I couldn't even tell you how many times I hit the man. He went down and he stayed down. That was all that mattered.

If the killer *was* a werewolf, they have a built-in toolkit for murder. But, if they were like me and far less rational about the situation, there were plenty of closer weapons at hand. There were tools on the outdoor barbeque. A few poker sticks for the fire pit. Several blunt objects. And the aforementioned kitchen knives.

This had to be deliberate. Right? I mean, why deliberately choose the silver knife and not something less... cliché?

"Have we considered Henry is being set up?" I asked, wondering why none of us would think of it earlier. "He's the only non-magical person involved in this. Everyone else is either werewolf or wizard. Maybe they thought Henry wouldn't know any better about silver?"

"Stabbing is a very mundane way to kill someone," Gerald agreed, as if such things were below him. He started to remind me of a dragon I know, and that's... not a compliment.

"Then why did Henry confess?" Ross pointed out, then turned to Phil. "Is there anything magical going on here?"

Phil sighed, like he didn't want to do it on the off chance he discovered something that did implicate Henry. But as Ross suspected, Phil was Phil, not me. He'd report the facts and then try to figure out how they supported his belief in his brother's innocence.

I nudged Ryan because I had an idea, a good one, for once. "Check all the doors, locks, any wards. Everything in the house. If so much as the breadbox was jimmied, I wanna know."

"On it." He slunk away and back into the house.

"Not even going to ask permission?" Gerald asked me.

"Nope." I smiled. "But I am gonna ask, if werewolves have such highly advanced senses of smell, couldn't you tell who killed Walter?"

Gerald let out a low growl and crossed his arms. "We had a very large party, plus much of the immediate family comes and goes as they please. We couldn't smell any person who didn't already have reason to be in the house."

"Is that why you sniffed us earlier?" I asked.

"Yes." He gave a very annoyed sigh. "I was hoping if I had your scents I might find it here, weak, but just below the surface."

Of course he wouldn't have smelled us because we didn't kill Walter. But this did mean that the killer was someone Walter knew, who had reason to be over at the house. Henry certainly fit that bill. So did Clara, who watched the proceedings with interest.

She didn't look afraid, like Phil might find something that would be incriminating against her. All I could see was apprehension. A need for answers.

"Nothing," Phil announced. "There is no trace of magic in the vicinity. If someone used a spell, then they would have to be deftly skilled in a way that I've never seen before."

"And he's seen a lot of shit," I reminded everyone.

"It still doesn't mean Henry did it," Phil was quick to keep defending his brother. "It could have easily been another human, or a werewolf."

"Or a magic user not using their magic," Ross countered.

"I—"

"Relax." She held her hand up. "I'm simply making a point. You have a solid alibi, along with Miss Masterson and Mr. Thompson."

"Henry didn't do this," Clara said as she stared down at the dark patch in the soil where Walter had bled out.

"Well," Gerald said, gesturing widely. "This was a waste of all our time."

"I wouldn't speak so soon." Ryan poked his head out the door. "Walter's desk—I assume his desk—has been broken into."

"No it hasn't," Gerald immediately countered, but it didn't sound like he was trying to cover up anything.

"Trust me, someone forced the lock."

If Ryan said a lock was jimmied, then it was. "Show us."

We all piled back into the house and made our way to the room. Unlike the study in Clara's house, which was used for multiple family members, this one was clearly a shrine to Walter Blakesley's ego. The walls where covered in all manner of awards and certificates. I assumed that even if he had kids, their photos still wouldn't have been up there.

"This one, here," Ryan pointed to the bottom right drawer.

"Looks secure to me," Gerald said as he squatted down to look at it more directly.

"Someone used a long piece of metal on it to pop the lock," Ryan explained. "And recently. There are fresh scrapings."

Gerald rubbed his thumb over it. "Huh, you're right."

"Duh."

"Open it," Ross ordered even though I'm pretty sure she'd need a warrant or something. Not that I was going to point that out. I was just as curious as to what was inside.

"I have uncle's keys," Gerald mumbled, reaching into his pocket. After a few minutes of finding the right one—and Ryan resisting the urge to just push him over and pick the lock himself—the drawer opened.

Annnnnnnnnnd… it was empty.

"Wasn't me!" Ryan immediately said.

"I'm noting a theme here," Ross said dryly.

Gerald stuck his head right over the empty drawer and took in several deep breaths through his nose. This would have weirded me out if I didn't know he was a werewolf.

"Smells like…" he took a minute to think about it. "Smells like paper, but blueprint paper. And old. There's some mold and dust that only comes from age."

"*Le Bosquet d'Argus.*" I blurted out, specifically at Clara. "The geographical data for *Le Bosquet d'Argus* was missing from your paperwork. And if this was old blueprint like paper, it could be the original land deeds and geographic maps, farm blueprints, shit like that."

Clara shook her head. "Everything we had was new."

"So someone has gone around and taken all the paperwork they can find on it." I'm no werewolf but this definitely smelled of a coverup. What was it about the farm that someone wanted to keep so well hidden that they would murder two people? Although, it wasn't exactly hidden anymore. The murders kind of brought attention to it. Was that unintentional?

"But there was nothing at *Le Bosquet*," Gerald reminded me. "Well, nothing we could immediately find, anyway. We do need to explore the barn once we can get past the debris."

"I'm just pointing out the coincidence." I'm not really a fan of them. Not since we misplaced Delaware that one time. "As in it's not, and this had to be deliberate."

"What is *Le Bosquet d'Argus*?" Ross asked because, yeah, she wasn't there for that.

"It's a farm our family owns," Clara explained. "It was abandoned long ago. But Uncle Walter was interested in taking over the land since the previous deed owner passed away a few months back."

"It's worth looking into," Ross decided quickly, as if she was happy to finally have something tangible to work with. "Miss Masterson, can you please return with Miss Blakesley to her house and check again if there is any information regarding the *Le Bosquet d'Argus*? We're going to stay here and see if we can find any trace of these missing papers."

"Sure." I didn't mind, I was just as curious as to where the missing paperwork went as she was.

I followed Clara back to the front of Walter's house. She seemed pretty lost in thought. It could have been the shock of actually standing where her uncle was murdered. It's one thing to know something happened, a whole other to be confronted with physical evidence of the act. Or maybe she had a thought and it weighed down on her.

I was going to ask her about it, but my phone beeped.

"I'm heading back, where are you right now?"

"Walter's. Heading back to Clara's house."

"See you in a few."

We got about six steps out of the house when Clara stopped suddenly. "You smell that?"

I reflexively sniffed but my olfactory senses are average for a not-werewolf. "Smell what?"

"Oh, no." Clara took off at a dead run.

Werewolves are fast. That's a given. But apparently this applies to them both in wolf and human form. Now, I'm a pretty hardcore runner. It's one of my hobbies to just run around Central Park—one day I'm going to try to race in a marathon—and even I couldn't keep up with the woman. At least I could still see her.

Others started to walk out of their houses as we ran past them towards Clara's. They smelled the same thing Clara had.

When I could see the house, I practically ran into a wall of the smell.

Smoke.

Clara's house was on fire.

"LUKE!" Clara screamed, running up to the door.

The fire hadn't reached the front of the house, otherwise her next move could have killed her. She opened the front door, allowing a fresh wave of air to rush in, fueling the fire. It caused a backdraft, but it didn't have the strength to get all the way down the entry hall and reach her. She started to gingerly walk inside, hand over her nose and mouth.

I'm not known for my decision-making skills, or my self-preservation skills, so of course I followed her right in. "Clara!"

"It's Luke!" she called back. "He's in the living room."

A living room that was blocked by a flaming hallway. The heat was so intense I had to consciously think about siphoning it to keep myself from getting overcome. Clare was sweating hard, hair matted to her face.

I grabbed her by the arm and shouted over the roar of the fire. "You can't get through that!"

"He's still alive!" She seemed very sure and I didn't know if it was due to her heighten senses or wishful thinking.

"You won't be if you try to go through that!" The hall was a wall of fire, feeding off the wood.

Clara wasn't listening to reason and things were only going to get worse. So I did what I had to. Using my grip on her arm… I tased her.

Sending electricity through her body, I held back on the amps so as not to kill her outright. Voltage to amperage is a very important ratio. And now that she was immobilized, I let her fall over my shoulder like a sack of potatoes. She'd thank me later.

I hoped.

I ran back outside with her, and by that time there was a large crowd of people gathered on the lawn. The gang was all there. One of the cops was on his radio. There was a bunch of people I hadn't seen before, residents of the other houses.

Wait, why I am describing this to you?

You were there, right?

You must have seen me kneel onto the grass so I could flip Clara off my shoulder with everyone's help. You probably heard her mumbling for her brother, saying his name over and over again. She needed to save him…

Odds are, he was already dead.

I know it.

You know it.

But I haven't let that stop me before.

I grabbed at Ryan's loose scarf, sliding it off.

And I ran back into the house.

SEVENTEEN[17]

Minni had ran the simulation a dozen times and it still wasn't working with optimal efficiency. At this point she was very much considering taking a fire axe to the computer.

"You'll burn a hole in it if you keep staring at your screen like that," her coworker, Gary, said from the cubicle next to hers.

"Maybe it'll set off the fire extinguishers?" Minni quipped back cheerfully.

"But I'm having a good hair day," he deadpanned back.

Minni chuckled and rubbed her eyes, taking a moment. Gary was about to become a grandfather but had never quite mastered the dad-joke, not that he didn't try his best. So what did that say about her state of mind that she actually laughed?

Her cellphone rang, or more accurately, vibrated on the desk. Taking personal calls during work wasn't prohibited, but Minni tried to be the best employee she could. She was the newest addition to the department, and the only woman. There was a burden on her to do well, whether or not any of her coworkers would admit it. Which they staunchly never did.

The caller ID came up as Laurence Harper, a name she didn't recognize. It could be anything from a wrong number to a spam call. Either way, she needed a break.

Grabbing the phone, she stood up and walked down the line of cubicles towards the back where there were a few empty offices. "Yell-o."

"Is this Minni Masterson?" the caller sounded serious.

"Why?" she answered back as she closed the door to an empty office behind her.

"I'm Detective Harper, 34th Precinct," the man introduced himself. "I'm a friend of Phil's."

"Oh," she didn't know quite how to respond to that. Why would a detective be calling her, and what did it have to do with Phil? "Is he okay?"

"Yes, he's fine, but he needs your help," Harper explained, urgency in his voice. "Can you give me your address? I'll come pick you up."

"Help with what?" Her paranoia crept up on her. Minni didn't know this guy, and just because he said he was Phil's friend didn't make it true. And just because he said he was a cop didn't make that true either, nor did it really help his case.

There was an exasperated sigh followed by mumbling and shuffling. Phil was then on the line. "Minni, it's Phil. Just get here now, okay?"

"Ah…" Minni didn't have a chance to respond. Someone—probably Phil—handed the phone back to Harper before Phil's magic shorted it out.

"We're in a bit of a hurry," Harper told her.

"Right, um, are you in a cop car or an unmarked car?"

"Unmarked…" He seemed thrown by the question.

"Okay, cool." Minni didn't want to be seen getting into a cop car outside her work building. Granted, the building was twelve stories and held several other businesses, but it was like a small village. Minni could learn all the details about the personal lives of people she had never actually met simply by forgetting to put her earbuds in while going up the elevator.

She gave Harper her work address, which was on 35th street, but he was up in Washington Heights. Normally it's a half hour drive but even unmarked cars have lights and sirens. He promised he would turn them off as he got closer.

"Hey, Boss?" Minni asked as she rapped on the door frame of his office and stuck her head in.

"Yes, Minni?" he asked as he looked up from his own computer. The man had worked for the company longer than Minni had been alive. It showed on his face with concentration permanently wrinkling his forehead and a pair of black-rimmed specs.

"Do you mind if I take an early and long lunch today?" she asked a bit timidly. "I need to run an errand and, frankly, I need to step away from the Patterson project before I take an axe to my computer."

Minni hadn't meant to say that last part out loud, but she couldn't take it back. The man simply chuckled and told her it was no problem.

After closing up the programs she was in, she headed downstairs, then out of a rather plain looking door onto the street. The bottom floor of the building was some kind of sports and recreation clothing store. It had large display windows complete with mannequins wearing the latest in thermo-control designs. She had worked in the building for almost a year now and had never once gone inside.

And she had yet to really get used to the noise of the city. Men worked with tools on the building next door, scaffolding climbing the façade like ivy. It wasn't lunchtime yet, but there was still plenty of people walking down the sidewalk, most in too much of a hurry for everyone around them. One day she'd walk out of the office and not even notice. Jury was still out if that would be a good thing.

A navy blue unmarked cop car pulled up, double parking. Minni walked up as the window rolled down. A black gentleman with a buzzed haircut poked his head out. "You Minni?"

"Most days," she replied.

"Hop in." He gestured to the rear driver's door.

Her paranoia crept up on her again, and instead she ran around to the other side to get into the front passenger's seat. The middle console was decked out with a computer and monitor, and a lot of extra bells and whistles. It was all shut off. Minni got the feeling that none of what was happening, or about to happen, was police sanctioned. Not that this surprised her in any way.

"Where we going?" she asked.

"One second," he replied as he pulled back into traffic.

Minni took the moment to poke at Harper's aura. Focusing her third eye, she could see the layers of energy that surrounded the man. Some of it was bio-electrical and some was from his consciousness creating its own unique energy field. But there was another layer there, one of magic. Only those born with the ability to use magic had it. It was the part of their aura, what they dipped into when trying to perform spells.

Harper's was quiet and… soft.

"You're a Forsaken," Minni practically blurted out.

"On my mother's side, yeah." He turned on the siren after they were a respectful distance from her office building. The moment the other cars started to get out of his way, Harper drove as fast as he could manage. They were on the Henry Hudson Parkway in what felt like record time.

Considering how fast he drove, and the traffic he was dodging, Minni elected not to ask further questions which might distract him.

When they exited the Parkway, Harper turned off the siren. They didn't have far to go. They parked in front of a two-story building surrounded by scaffolding, construction signs, and a banner denoting premium office space was coming soon. Plastic sheeting hung from the scaffolds and swayed gently in the breeze, the area eerily quiet.

"Okay, before we go in there," Minni said as Harper pulled aside some plastic, "I just want to remind you that I am a witch—granted, not a very good one—but I can create a bolt of lightning at will."

Harper looked back at her frowned. "Are you threatening a police officer?"

"Yes." Minni didn't even try to walk it back. "I don't know you and this looks dodgy as hell. And I think you of all people should understand why people who look like us don't trust cops."

The man opened his mouth, but immediately gave up on any retort he might have. What could he say against the truth?

Ryan poked his head out. "Minni! Get in here, quick."

Minni didn't hesitate, pushing past Harper to follow Ryan into the building. They passed through a hallway that was only framing missing its sheetrock.

When they finally got the heart of the building, the only term Minni could think of was 'gutted.' The entirety of the inside structure was gone save some support pillars holding up a roof that was spotted with holes. The second floor was gone and the first floor was down to the concrete. It looked like the builders kept the façade but were completely redoing the interior.

That was the first thing Minni noticed.

The second was all the floating people.

"What the….?" Minni said under her breath.

Five individuals in the sixteen-to-twenty age bracket were currently experiencing gravitational disruptions. One held onto a rope attached to a plumping pipe to keep themselves from flying off. Two were stuck up underneath the bottom section of a piece of scaffolding. One held onto a cement mixer for dear life, though it looked like a rope had been tied around their waist and attached to the machine. The last one clung to a metal beam which ran between two pillars, a remnant of the second floor that once was.

All looked absolutely terrified.

"Long story short," Ryan said as he pointed to a small ritual circle, complete with incense and candles. "Don't play with magic unless you know what you're doing."

Minni looked at the circle, looked up at one of the floating people, then back to the circle, making note that even she could tell the symbols were a mishmash that made no sense. She glanced at Ryan. "How…?"

"No time for that." Phil walked into the expanse, dragging a mattress that he might have literally just dumpster dived for. "We need to break the spell."

"Why am I worried about your use of the word *we*?"

Ryan helped to lug the mattress under the unlucky one who was holding onto the beam. Everyone else didn't have to far to fall once the spell broke. And a one-story fall onto concrete isn't guaranteed to kill you, but odds were you wouldn't be happy after you hit the ground. Phil left Ryan to position the mattress carefully and went back to Minni. "They each cast the spell, it wasn't area of effect. I have to break them one by one."

"Oh…" Minni did the math in her head. To properly break a spell without damage to the caster or the breaker takes time. Hours. And there were five of them. "I don't know how I can help. You know I don't know how to properly break spells. Don't you have someone else you can call?"

"Minni." Phil took a breath and chose his words. "You are the fastest solution here. I break the spells, the quick and dirty way, which is going to cause a very large magical discharge that you will siphon off."

"No, no no nononono." Minni put her hands up, backing off. "That size of a discharge could—correction—*would* fry you."

"But not you. You can grab it, funnel it off."

"Five broken spells worth?" Minni laughed incredulously.

"You can do it."

"You don't know that!"

Phil took another breath, stepping slightly closer so he could lower his voice and still be heard. "Minni, you transferred a man's complete lifeforce into to your brother. We both know that's a lot heavier lifting than what I'm asking you to do."

Minni's throat and jaw tightened. "That was different."

"Yes it was," he replied simply. "It was harder."

She looked away, past all the rebar and into the void that slowly followed her wherever she went.

"Minni," Phil said softly. "Help me save these kids."

"Fine," Minni snapped back at him. "But if you die that one is *not* on me."

"I won't die. I know you can do this."

Minni wanted to believe him. She also wanted to punch him. A glare would have to do for a compromise.

"Ready here," Ryan called out and Phil's attention went back to the task at hand. He gestured for Minni to follow him over to the ritual circle.

"Okay Minni, I want you to sit behind me," he said as he sat cross-legged on the concrete. "When I break the spell, catch the backlash like a lightning rod. I'll have to do each one separately so that should give you time to process the incoming magic."

"Sure." Minni didn't sound very convinced, but she sat down as instructed anyway.

"Ready?" Phil asked after a moment.

Minni took a long breath and opened her third eye again so she could see the magic swirling around the unlucky wannabe wizards. It was lightweight, feathery even, dancing along the air. Almost peaceful. "Yeah, I'm ready."

"Okay, we'll start from the top and work our way down." Phil closed his eyes and took a deep breath. His aura began to undulate as he dipped into it to pull out his magic. Wild and spikey, his aura was typical of a wizard who used their magic often. Every time they touched their aura it caused a ripple which would grow into waves, crashing against each other until a perfect storm always raged across it. Lightning constantly illuminated it.

In perfect contrast, Minni's aura was quiet and tame. When she reached for her magic, it was like an Olympic high diver, controlled and smooth, barely a splash. It had always been that way. It was years before she realized that this kind of control wasn't the norm. That wizards weren't naturally able to simple *feel* the energy, slice through it like a scalpel, and bend it to their will. The long faces of her parents when they realized what she could do was her first clue that this wasn't a blessing, but a curse.

"Ita est finis," Phil called out as he completed his breaking spell on the poor soul holding onto the beam.

Wizards may be born with magic, but it is a force that wizards use only by its good grace. It's a symbiotic relationship that can easily turn sour. When a wizard tries to break a spell, even a spell cast by someone of lesser strength than them, the result is the same. In basic terms, magic gets pissed, turning feral and violent because you upset what it was meant—what it was *made*—to do.

A powerful wave of magical energy screamed towards Phil, heating the air around it and crackling ions throughout the room. Had it hit Phil, it would have literally shorted him out. The magic would have latched onto his aura and start ripping it apart at the subatomic level. Phil's brain would scramble, the bioelectric neurons misfiring at a rapid pace. He would be thrown into a coma that he *might* wake up from. Eventually.

Minni reached out and grabbed the magic like a snake charmer unafraid to grip a cobra by its neck. It lashed out, trying to morph and destabilize itself to slip out of her grasp. Minni simply let it try, wrapping a thin coat of her own magic around it like steel cellophane to keep it from breaking away. Then slowly she drew it in, absorbed it into her own aura easily as if she was breathing air into her lungs.

But this air was gritty and putrid. If it were food, it would be spoiled. This was someone else's magic, someone else's spell. It didn't belong to her.

"Got it, Minni?" Phil asked.

"Yeah, kinda nauseous, but yeah."

"Next?"

Minni took a deep, cleansing breath. "Do it."

Phil began the process again, this time with the person holding onto the rope. The first kid had fallen safely onto the mattress and Ryan was tending to them. Harper stood back, letting the magic users do their thing.

"Ita est finis," Phil said again and another wave of angry magic shot towards them.

Snatching it like the one before, Minni pulled the magic inside her aura, caging it with the other. Her body started to feel weird, like the returning sensation of gravity after being in a pool for a long time. Everything just felt heavier for the moment because you were used to weightlessness.

"Next." Phil kept going, assuming she'd say something if they needed to stop.

Minni probably should have sad something. This wouldn't be the first (nor the last) time that Minni's tendency to just take the brunt of the pain and work through it would get her into trouble.

They broke the spell on the kid holding onto the cement mixer next. Ryan stood by to keep them from braining themselves on the machine. Then they moved onto the two stuck under the scaffolding. Phil started with the one the right. They pretty much just had to step down, holding onto one of the bars of the structure to swing rather than fall.

"Last one," Phil said with a measure of relief.

All the formed magic swirled inside of Minni's aura, fighting her at every step. It didn't want to be contained. She wasn't its master. Minni worried all of it would manifest into something solid and crawl up her throat to get out.

"Ita est finis," Phil broke the final spell and the magic screamed forth. Minni caught it, wrestled it, and dragged it inside her aura with the rest.

Minni didn't feel heavy anymore.

In fact, she felt lighter than air. It was actually a nice sensation, no pressure on any of her joints. The crick in her neck from staring at her computer screen for too long had worked its way loose. Her spine wasn't aching from being hunched over and compressed. Then there was the vice-like bans around her middle.

"Minni!" Phil shouted.

She blinked rapidly, clearing her vision of her Third Eye to see the reality of the situation. No longer sitting on the floor, she floated, the gravity spell having taken root. It snuck into the cracks of her aura and pressed against the forces holding her to the Earth. It was going to have its way, it was wasn't meant to be locked down.

"I got her." Harper had his arms wrapped around Minni's torso from behind to keep her grounded.

Minni began to shake, her breaths coming in shallow bursts. The magic was everywhere, screaming in her ears. It was going to consume her, she knew it. She would either end up flying into the stratosphere or pulled apart, molecule by molecule, until it got what it wanted.

"Minni, listen to me." Phil was right beside her. "You need to take a deep breath. In and out. Can you do that for me?"

She tried to breathe but she could only choke. Her body was paralyzed, but not by magic. She'd gone too far, done too much. There had to be a limit, there was always a limit. Minni was now frightened that she just found hers and was paying the price.

"In and out, Minni. In… and out."

Slowing her breaths did nothing to combat the fear that swept through her like an artic snowstorm, seizing up her mind as well as her body.

"You're stronger than it, Minni," he told her with firm declaration. "You can control it."

"I can't." Minni shook her head, fighting back tears. "I can't hold onto it."

"Then don't."

Minni sharply looked down at him.

"You drew it in, you can throw it out." The absolute faith he had in her was terrifying. "Put it someplace where it can't hurt anyone."

Someplace it couldn't hurt anyone. Any*thing*.

Taking another deep breath, Minni closed her eyes and wrestled with the magic. It was stronger than anything Minni had dealt with before. She mustered whatever faith she could that she would win against it. That she was stubborn enough to try. Focusing on the fight, she dragged it kicking and screaming from every inch of her aura, surprising herself.

It... it couldn't be that easy.

Minni held the magic in a death-grip, but if she took too long it would surely seep back into her and tear her apart. Eyes snapping open, the first thing Minni saw was one of the candles used to perform the spell. The magic found it… familiar. She put her left hand out and threw the magic away with all her strength, right into the candle. It wailed like a banshee, but returned home.

The candle shot up into the air like a rocket, hitting the roof. It then rolled a few feet to one of the pockmarked holes and disappeared into the sky. It may never come back down.

Minni slumped in Harper's arms, again beholden to the forces of gravity. The detective lowered her to the ground, slowly letting go in case she started to fly off again. She pitched forward slightly and Phil grabbed her by the shoulders.

"You okay?" he asked.

"I hate you," she replied breathlessly.

"She's okay," Phil told everyone.

A moment later, she was sitting on an upturned cement block, bent over, trying not to throw up. Phil left her to recover and went to take care of the others. Ryan showed up a moment later and gave her a bottle of water. She gulped it down and tried to wash the nausea away.

"That was pretty badass," Ryan said.

Minni glanced up at him as if she wasn't sure if she should punch him.

"I'm serious," he defended his statement. "Phil couldn't have done that. I definitely couldn't have done that. I mean, I knew you were more powerful than you let on, but damn."

It was the last thing she wanted to hear. This was this very same 'badass power' that killed a man to save a brother who resented her for it. That the Council lorded over her, letting her know that she only lived at their leisure. Despite all this, Minni still loved being a witch, it was truly the only thing no one could take from her.

But there is no such thing as a good person, and they all had to pay a price for that.

"Do you need to go to the hospital?" Harper asked her.

"No, I'm okay." Minni took a deep breath and stood. She barely got light headed and considered that a win. "Can you take me back to work?"

"Are you sure?" He was using that policeman tone on her and maybe she wanted to punch him instead. She definitely wanted to punch *something*.

"Yes, I'm sure. My project isn't going to finish itself."

"Okay." Harper clearly didn't think she was up for it, but after what he just saw, he wasn't going to argue. He may not use his magic, but he knew enough to know what happened wasn't normal. That there was something special and very dangerous about Minni Masterson. "Oh, hey, uh, apologies for grabbing you like that. You started to float, and it took us by surprise."

"No worries, I appreciate it." She really didn't want to end up like that candle.

Minni easily convinced Harper to stop at a Dunkin' on the way back to work. By the time she rode the elevator up, most everyone else was returning from their normal lunch hour.

"You okay there, Minni?" her boss asked when he saw her. He stood at Gary's desk, chatting with him.

"Yeah," she said as she slumped into her chair, setting a bag of munchkins and a half-drunk latte down in front of her. "Just had to run to make several connecting buses."

"Oh, that's rough," Gary agreed.

Minni opened her computer programs and set herself back to the task of figuring out what was going wrong with the design. As she waited for everything to load, she reached out to feel the hum of electricity all around her. The current buzzed softly and it was soothing. It was like listening to a bubbling brook. She traced it all throughout the building, every junction box and loose cellphone.

In a single breath she could have drawn it all inside her, blacking out the building.

She could do it and no one could stop her.

EIGHTEEN[18]

Wednesday, January 31st, 2018
2:36am

Yeah, I don't know why no one stopped me, or what I was thinking, running back into the house like that, tying Ryan's scarf around my nose and mouth. Although, some of them did yell at me to stop, but I learned to tune that shit out a long time ago. I knew what I was doing.

And I just keep doing it anyway.

Now, here is the thing about me. Yes, I am great at energy transfer and I can light a candle at thirty paces. But a fire is more than just thermal energy and a house fire is a lot more than your average Yankee Candle. If my talent was only fire and that's all I ever focused on, like Eli and Viv, then yeah, I could probably command the blaze to settle its little ass down and behave. Unfortunately, fire is not really my talent. Phil doesn't have the expertise, either. Anything that Phil could do wouldn't be in a time frame that would matter to Luke.

The fire had grown, still blocking the hallway and entrance into the living room. It was hotter than hell and again I had to mentally concentrate on siphoning off the heat. Smoke filled the air and I seriously had second thoughts for a moment. But it's been brought to my attention recently that sometimes... something just kind of snaps in me.

I ran towards the wall of fire.

I couldn't make a solid shield to part through the flames because that would just mean a backdraft would lick around it. Also, not a smart idea to try and draw in the thermal energy while actually standing in the flames themselves. My clothes, hair, skin—everything, really—could easily become fuel due to the combustion reactions. That's far too much to try to control at once.

159

So instead, I took a deep breath, and created a solid wall of energy around myself. This wall had to be tight enough to make sure that oxygen couldn't get in, otherwise the flames would follow the fuel source. Key phrase there: oxygen couldn't get in.

I stepped quickly through the fire, hoping that I wasn't about to step into a hole or just more flames. Thankfully, while the center of the living room was layered in smoke and a chair was on fire--as was parts of the ceiling--the floor looked to be mostly untouched for the moment.

I could barely see Luke through the haze. He lay on his side between the sofa and the coffee table. I bent down beside him and realized I'd been essentially holding my breath for too long. I had to slowly let the oxygen in and push the carbon dioxide out to keep from attracting the fire to me. The flames were far enough away that once I got air back, it was only the smoke I had to worry about.

That's why I took Ryan's scarf. It was better than nothing.

I turned Luke onto his back to check his vitals. I'm not a doctor but his pulse was a thing that was still happening and his chest rose, barely. My best guess was he was suffering from smoke inhalation and wasn't going to wake up any time soon. I was just about to haul him over my shoulder to carry him out when I heard it.

Timbers cracked as the ceiling started to cave in. I threw myself over Luke but thankfully the subfloor above us remained intact, for now. The sucky part was that the hallway was now blocked as it had been taking most of the brunt of the fire. You know, I wonder if that new construction they did to remodel made it more susceptible?

My entrance no longer my egress, I looked around for any other possible means of escape. The front window was blocked, a piano on fire in front of it. I couldn't see the back door in the kitchen from where I was. There were no guarantees that it wasn't blocked as well. If it was, then I would trap myself and waste precious time trying to save us. So I could either risk it, or I could just blow the whole thing up.

Hey, so, fun fact: did you know they put out oil well fires by setting off an explosion at their base?

"Take a deep breath," I told Luke, though he probably couldn't hear me.

I built the energy wall around me again, the one that wouldn't let oxygen through. Once I had it sturdy… I pushed. I spread it out in a dome shape, pressing through every void and crack, snuffing the life from even the most stubborn of timbers. There was no more oxygen to fuel the flames within the barrier. Within seconds the house was now encased in a vacuum filled bubble, like a snow globe. No noise, no fire, and no air.

This, this was the easy part.

I had to bring the bubble back slowly, methodically quelling the fires that wanted to start back up once the embers touched air again. It was an agonizing pace, in more ways than one. My lungs began to burn as I used up what oxygen I was able to pull in when I created the shield. I started to miss some of the smaller hot spots and hoped that they would behave themselves long enough for the fire fighters to take care of them.

At least, I hoped there were fire fighters out there by now. Otherwise I was screwed.

I could feel the flames, almost sentient, try to restart and consume. They spoke to me, telling me a story of how they came to be and why they should be allowed to flourish. They were brought fourth, invited out of the fireplace to climb the wall and dance across the ceiling. They were *invited*.

I could hear them shouting, clamoring to return to their glory. They were meant to react, to combust, to breathe heat and smoke. I could hear them scream 'how dare I keep that from them?'

Or it could have been the hypoxia setting in.

My shield was about ten feet from me when my body gave out. Oxygen rushed in as the barrier collapsed. I gasped for air, looking around to be sure that the house was no longer on fire and there was no immediate threat.

Then I promptly passed out.

This magic shit is hard.

NINETEEN[19]

When I woke up, I was laying on a stretcher with a fire fighter standing over me, pressing an oxygen mask to my face. I glanced over see Luke up on a gurney, getting the same treatment. The house fire was pretty much out, but the other fire fighters were pouring water on it, just in case. I didn't see you anywhere, so I don't think you were present for this. Stop me if I can skip over anything.

Anyway, I let myself take a few more hits of pure oxygen and then gave the guy a thumbs up. I hadn't really breathed in a lot of smoke, just not a lot of air.

"Thanks," I said to the fireman and propped myself up. The guy did another check of my vitals.

"Minni!" Uncle James came over and squatted down next to me. "How you doing?"

"Oh, I'm fine," I said with a sarcastic smile.

"That's good," he said with relief. "You mother would have killed me if anything happened to you."

I frowned at him. "Why would she? It's not like you could have done anything to prevent it." I mean, I did run into the house by my own free will, and he wasn't even there yet.

"Do you think that would stop your mother?"

"You make an excellent point." Well, I had to give him that one. "How's Luke?"

"Thankfully pretty okay, just regained consciousness." He gestured over at Luke who was laying on a gurney, a paramedic working on him. "A werewolf's healing powers also transfer to their human form. He'll still have to go to the hospital, but a full recovery is just a matter of time at this point."

"And he's going to have a lot of it," I mumbled.

"What?"

I turned to the fire fighter. "I'm good?"

"Yeah," he said, putting away the oxygen tank. "But if you feel any lightheadedness or have difficulty in breathing, you want to get checked out."

"Thanks," I said, then Uncle James helped me to stand.

We headed over to Luke who was surrounded by pretty much everyone involved in this mystery. Clara was there, holding his hand, the picture of the distraught sister. Phil was next to her, pensive as always. Ryan was off to the side, rocking slightly on his feet from both the cold and not really knowing what to do with himself. Agent Ross stood at the end of the gurney looking stone faced. Gerald and Declan stood off to the other side, both curious, but that was the only emotion I could read on them. Detective Longtree was asking Luke questions while the EMTs worked behind him to ready the ambulance to take him to the hospital.

"You don't know how the fire started?" Longtree was saying to Luke. "Did you see, hear, or smell anyone?"

"No, sorry, I wasn't paying attention," Luke answered.

Now, when approaching sensitive situations, it's best to take a diplomatic approach to these things. So I cleared my throat and said, "That's because you were too busy setting the fire."

I said diplomatic was the *best* choice.

I think we've established that I don't do that.

Clara did a double-take at me. "I'm sorry, what?"

"Luke set the fire," I stated more exactly.

"Ah, Minni." Phil looked at me like he knew I wouldn't be lying about something like this, but clearly I must be mistaken. "The fire was already going before you got there.

"Yes, it started in the fireplace," I explained, turning to Luke. "You were found five feet from it. Now, I'm not an expert, I admit that, but you couldn't have been overcome with smoke that fast, being a werewolf. If the fire was *that bad* when you got to it, it would have been impossible for you to get into the living room without at least singeing your clothes."

Everyone took that in, but Longtree asked, "How do you know it started in the fireplace?"

"It told me."

Longtree looked like he was going to question me on that but then decided better of it. Instead he turned back to Luke. "Did you set the fire?"

Luke could have lied. If he was a good enough liar, then everyone might have believed him over me. Hell, I might have believed him over me. I was kind of shooting from the hip there. But Luke either saw the writing or the wall or was too tired of running. "Yes, I set the fire."

"Why?" Clara asked, voice shaky.

"I just wanted all this to be over," he admitted, not daring to look at her.

You could almost feel the collective force of all the cogs clicking into place in Clara's head. She figured it out. "Luke? What did you do?" Clara nearly pleaded, as if hoping she was wrong and he would clear up what was of course a misunderstanding.

When he didn't answer, well, I've already mentioned I'm a lousy diplomat. "He murdered Walter, he murdered Aunt Lori, and then tried to burn the evidence, including himself."

Okay, now that I think back on the moment, that was highly insensitive. I may have needed a few more hits of oxygen.

"No, no no no." Clara grabbed her brother by the face and continued to plead with him.

All Luke did was sob, "I'm sorry," over and over again.

"Why did he do it?" Phil asked, everyone else looking to me for answers.

"I don't know," I admitted. "I just figured out that he did it. I have no idea *why* he did it."

"And just how *did* he do it?" Longtree asked.

"He stayed behind after Phil was arrested and the party broke up." It was the only thing that made sense once I worked backwards from what I discovered while rescuing Luke. "That, or he doubled back. Either way, he stole the paperwork and stabbed Walter, not necessarily in that order. A little help Luke?"

He completely ignored me, the siblings still holding each other and crying.

"That's a no then." His confirmation would have made me feel more confident, but then he hadn't denied anything I said so far. "Now, whatever led Luke to kill Water must have led him to Aunt Lori."

"When I interviewed Luke earlier," Agent Ross spoke up, "he said he'd been at Lori Blakesley's before coming back to the house, but well before she died. Her medication could have been tampered with at any point."

"But why kill Aunt Lori?" Ryan asked. "What does she have to do with *Le Bosquet*?"

"It wasn't that," Gerald said gravely, a pensive look on his face, as if he was holding back from attacking Luke until he understood why the man did it. "Nothing significant happens in this sub-pack without Aunt Lori's approval. So whatever Walter did to warrant his death, she was very likely culpable as well."

"She could have wanted Luke to turn himself in," Declan offered, but even he didn't seem to believe it.

"She would have never let him leave the house."

"I kinda figured as much," I said quietly. I mean, I didn't take werewolves as the type to just let Luke walk away after admitting to a murder. I felt both proud I'd figured everything out, and a little awful that I was proud.

Ryan raised his hand. "I still don't understand what any of this has to do with *Le Bosquet d'Argus*."

"It had to do with the soil, right?" I asked Luke, though I don't know why I thought he would answer me when he couldn't form any words to speak to his sister. "There's no mercury. That was a lie to keep people from digging, to hide something in the soil that you could smell with your super-sniffer."

"We don't really like that term," Gerald said bluntly.

"Oh, sorry."

"Did you feel them?" Luke asked, surprising everyone. His glassy eyes turned towards me as if in some kind of plea to let him know he wasn't crazy. "Did you feel them, in the ground?"

"Um…" I thought back to when I did my interpretation of ground penetrating radar. I was looking for mercury or other metals. I wasn't really paying attention to the normal shit you find in the ground. Or in some cases, what you don't find. "Voids. There were a few voids of not as densely packed earth with a different electrical resistance level, but it wasn't metal. More like something had been buried and… decomposed."

"Decomposed." Longtree looked at me squarely. "As in in human remains?"

He wanted me to be clear, so I did my best. "The voids were not small-or medium-sized. So, either human or a large animal, like a werewolf…"

"Holy shit," Ryan said under his breath, but it had gotten so quiet that even with the emergency vehicles and firefighters moving around we could all hear him.

"Let me make sure I understand this," Agent Ross spoke suddenly, almost making me jump. "There are unknown persons buried out at this farm long enough ago to be completely decomposed. A farm owned by Walter and Lori's brother until his recent death. A farm that had been declared poisoned and unfit for use. A farm that Walter wanted, presumably to continue to keep it vacant."

"What are you saying?" Gerald snapped at Agent Ross.

"I'm saying there is conspiracy to cover-up the deaths of those unknown persons," Agent Ross said as if she was wishing she was at home still in bed, because it was entirely too late for this. "Typically, that means murder."

"What are you accusing Uncle Walter of?" Gerald asked, clearly in denial, hoping someone will give him the answer that isn't so obviously in front of him.

"He admitted it." Luke said, his voice breaking even more than I thought possible. "Right before the party. Told me I just had to accept things the way they are."

Yeah, I don't know what he was referring to, but it got really crowded and loud as Gerald tried to defend his uncle. Longtree tried to keep bloodshed from occurring while also belatedly telling Luke his rights so he could arrest him. Agent Ross was also trying to keep the peace, along with Phil. Clara looked like she might turn wolf to protect her brother regardless.

I was pretty sure I had done enough, both good and bad, and took a few steps back. I ended up stumbling and sat down on this concrete bench that was at the edge of the neighbor's yard.

"You okay?" Ryan asked me.

"I'm fine, just need some air." I pointed at Phil. "He's the one who's going to need help."

"I think all of them are," Ryan replied sadly, and it wasn't like I could argue with him on that one. Then he gestured to his scarf which was somehow still around my neck. "I'm never going to get the smoke smell out of that now."

"You have a million of them," I grumbled as I slid it off.

"That's not the point," he said as he took it. "And why did you need it anyway? Couldn't you just make a shield to filter out the smoke?"

I mean, I could have, if I had sat down long enough to build the spell into my focus bracelet. But unlike kinetic barriers and EMP pulses, I usually don't have a lot of use for a smoke barrier spell and kind of forgot I should do the thing. As for needing the scarf, well. "There is no way I was going to be able to make a smoke filter on the fly. And you know why? Oxygen is .0005 microns, carbon dioxide is .00065 microns. A micron is one-millionth of a meter by the way, and smoke particles are they themselves around one micron depending on their source and-- hey, where are you going?"

"There's already been enough trauma tonight," he said as he started walking back towards the group. "Don't need to add math to it."

I chuckled lightly, then took a few deep breaths. A bit of a mistake seeing as there was still some smoke in the air from the fire. But the adrenaline was washing out of my system and I was feeling it. When I'm in the moment, doing reckless shit, it's almost like instinct. Afterwards, once I come back to my senses, all I can do is focus on the fact that I made it through.

It was something I never really realized I did, not until recently. A dragon told me I should tempter my instincts to protect. I hate to admit that he might be right. But how does one go about not helping people? I suppose I could start by not making rash decisions all the time.

Instead of contemplating this, my thoughts turned to whether or not I should curl up on the bench and take a nap. That's when you trotted over and jumped up next to me, nudging me with that cold snout of yours. You glanced between the me and the house, your big puppy dog eyes all sad and shit.

"Okay, so the building may currently be a smoldering pile of ash, sure, but it was on fire when I got here. And, hey, I put it out; what more do you want from me?"

TWENTY[20]

Telling the story of what happened to the werewolf was a cathartic for Minni. Things happened, she acknowledged it, and now she could move on. If she didn't, if she dwelled, then this moment would turn into infected scabs on her psyche.

She knows she acts before she thinks, what done is done.

When Minni got into these moods she had a tendency to ramble, but the werewolf didn't seem to mind. They ended up curled next to Minni, head resting on her knee. Minni even gave them scratches behind the ears as she talked.

"Looks like order has been restored," Minni said, watching as EMTs loaded Luke into the ambulance, one of Longtree's officers riding along.

Phil and James led a crying Clara away. They put her in James' car but didn't immediately leave. They were all chatting about things Minni probably needed to hear, but she was too tired to get up. She'd deal with it later. That was her usual go-to plan.

"Hey." Declan walked over to where Minni was setting.

"Hey," Minni replied back. "Did he give a motive?"

"I couldn't really follow," he admitted, a defeated slump to his shoulders. "Something about him going out to *Le Bosquet d'Argus* a few weeks ago, after Uncle Jeremiah died. In his wolf form, his sense of smell is highly acute, moreso than the rest of us. He could smell the graves, some older, some newer, and… and one smelt like his mother."

"Ho-ly shit." Minni's thought processes stalled out. They had assumed their mom ran away. She was here the whole time, buried on a family-owned farm. "I don't even know where to start unraveling all of that."

"Yeah, it's, ah…" Declan stopped, giving up on words because he couldn't find ones accurate enough to express his feelings on the situation. "Yeah."

"Right." Minni took a deep breath and rubbed her hands on her legs. This caused the werewolf to sit up beside her. "Well, um, don't take this personally, Declan, but, I kinda just want to go home and not deal with… any of this."

"I feel guilty that I wish I had that luxury," Declan replied wryly. He scratched the back of his neck and thought for a moment. "Look, as messy as all this is, thank you. You saved Clara, and Luke… which is good, because now we know the truth and can start putting all the pieces together. No one else is going to say it, so… thank you."

"I don't think 'you're welcome' is the right term to use right now." Minni frowned, watching the ambulance leave with Luke. "Seems a bit trite."

"Yeah…"

"I should probably get back over there." Minni wasn't sure what plans Phil, James, or Ryan had at the moment. She only knew she had to go home at some point to get enough sleep to make it through work with minimal magic use. "I've probably talked this guy's ear off. Or girl? What's their name?"

"Axe," Declan said as he reached forward and started to scratch Axe around the ears and neck. "Though I think we need to rename him Houdini. He's gotten out of his collar again."

"Wait, wut? They're not a werewolf?"

"No, not even a wolf," Declan said as he continued to give him scratches. "He's a herd dog, a Lapponian."

"So… this is someone's pet?"

"Yes."

Minni looked between them. "You keep dogs as pets?"

"They're man's best friend." Declan scratched the ridge of Axe's nose and the dog's tail wagging happily, thumping against the bench.

Minni rubbed her forehead, mumbling, "I can't believe I've been talking to a dog this whole time."

"They're very good listeners."

"Not helping."

"I'll get Axe back home," Declan said, a slight chuckled to his voice. He patted his leg and Axe jumped off the bench to stand beside him, still happily wagging his tail. "Let me guess, you're a cat person?"

"I'm a nothing person," she replied wryly. "I have zero pets. Even as a kid none of the family pets were my own."

"I thought all witches had, um, familiars."

"A lot of witches had cats or birds or other pets, but because they were often outcasts and so... lonely." Minni let those words sink in a little too far. When she was cast out her home, imprisoned in New York City, she had been alone. "Anyway, nothing magical about it."

"Huh." Declan absently scratched Axe between the ears. "So that's why you don't have a pet, because you're not alone."

Minni tilted her head, not understanding what he meant.

"There's a metallic smell on you," Declan explained. "It's like... pennies, copper. It's a strong, well-worn smell that isn't yours. So a boyfriend, I take it?"

"Ah, yeah." Minni thought of Marcel who was would be up any minute now for his early ass morning shift. "So you're telling me I carry my boyfriend's scent?"

"And he probably carries yours."

Minni had to ask. "What do I smell like?"

"Um, well, I don't have all the notes, like Gerald would." Declan took a second to gather his thoughts. "You're metallic, too, but a lot more complex. It's like... a mix of copper and gold."

"Like... red gold?"

"What's red gold?"

"It's a gold/copper alloy, similar to rose gold but a lot more copper in it. Like fifty/fifty split," Minni said, trying to wrap the idea of smelling like red gold around her head. Especially as what we'd call a 'metallic smell' is actually the product of oils and other things reacting to the metal, and not from the metal itself. Which is what Declan must have been basing his observations on.

"Is it weird you know what red gold is?" Declan asked.

"My best friend is a New York City fashion designer."

"Yeah, that would do it."

Minni stood up, feeling achy but otherwise better than she had earlier. "Well, it was nice meeting you, just a shame about the murder… murders."

"You don't people well," he noted.

"No, no I do not." There was no denying the truth. "Take care of yourself."

"You, too." Declan patted his leg again and Axe perked up. "Come on, let's get you home."

Declan walked off, the dog happily bouncing along, completely unawares of the tragedy that was all around it. Or maybe he did know and was trying to cheer up all the sad people. It did make Minni smile for a moment.

Minni sent off a text to Marcel. *Text me when you get up. Peek-a-boo.*

Now there was nothing left to keep Minni from rejoining her friends and becoming a part of what was happening again. She walked over to where Phil, Ryan, and her Uncle James were chatting. Clara was laying down in the back seat of James' car. She'd been crying and may have possibly fallen asleep. Dreaming was probably better than the nightmare she was currently living.

"So." Minni put her hands in her pockets and rocked on her heels. "That was… something."

Phil and James gave her a blank look.

"Look, this is what happens when you make me be the adult." She was perfectly honest.

"As unfortunate as that statement is," Phil said wryly, "you did the right thing. Thank you."

"People need to stop thanking me or I'm gonna start getting a complex," Minni replied awkwardly. "Everything sorted out with your brother?"

"Yeah, Longtree is going to release him," Phil answered with a wealth of relief. "We need to head over there but someone needs to stay with Clara."

"Oh, right." Minni nodded. Not only had Clara's house been burned down, but her brother was responsible for the death of an elder and a pack-mother. Clara was probably persona-non-grata with her clan until the mess was sorted out.

Who were in the other graves? Why were they there in the first place? Obviously Jeramiah and Walter Blakesley knew about them, and the pack-mother. They were hiding a secret that was at least twenty years old. Who else knew?

Minni cleared her throat. "Uh, anything I can do?"

"Go with James to the police station. You'll also need to give a statement."

"Yeah." Minni sighed, weariness still sitting in her bones.

They piled into James' car, Clara sitting up and leaning on Phil. She was still sniffling, mumbling about what had happened, what could and couldn't be true. Minni tried to be as unobtrusive as possible.

"*I see you. I just got out of the shower,*" Marcel texted her. "*Have you gotten any sleep?*"

A shower sounded really nice to Minni right now. "*No, but soon… [zzz's emoji].*"

At the station, Minni was led in a room and given a legal pad. She was told to write out everything that happened, twice. One with all the details and one omitting anything magic related for the public records. She let Marcel finish getting ready to work and focused on getting everything written out as quickly as possible so she could go home.

"Hey." Minni stuck her head out of the door, getting Longtree's attention as he walked past. "So, how do I say that I walked through fire without admitting to magic?"

"Just say there was a narrow but open path."

It sounded like a good idea, but, "I, ah, I'm not going to be called back for any kind of trial, am I?"

"I really hope not." He kept walking. Minni wasn't sure if he was referring to the trial or the idea of ever seeing Minni again.

Halfway through finishing, she got a text. "*At work. The last shift left everything a mess. Just piles of incomplete paperwork.*"

"Assholes. Looks like we're both stuck doing paperwork atm."

"You're still awake? Doing paperwork?"

"Long story. Tell you later." Which was both a truth and a lie. Minni would indeed tell Marcel about Henry, the Blakesley's, the murders, and her rescue of Luke. But she'd downplay most of it, and of course not mention the magic aspect. But the thought of what *did* happen finally hit her as she stared down at her phone. *"Love you."*

The phone immediately began to ring.

"Hey," Minni answered.

"Are you okay?" Marcel asked.

"Yeah, I'm fine." She sat back in her chair. "There was a fire but I am okay, didn't get singed."

"A fire?" His voice was full of worry, but perhaps not as much as there could have been. If it was bad, if she was actually hurt beyond some scrapes and bruises, she would have called him right away. "Are you still with Phil?"

"Yeah, he and his brother are okay, too."

"Do you need me to come get you? I can take off work —"

"No, it's okay." And it would also be hard for her to explain how she got to Rome so quickly. "You get to sorting out that mess. I'll see you for your lunch."

There was a long slow breath on the other side of the line. She knew Marcel didn't like this, he never did, but Minni was... Minni. A few months ago she was attacked and almost died when a cultist tried to sacrifice her. That was the story she told Marcel. Either way, Minni had survived it, this was a piece of cake.

But there is such a thing as too much cake.

"Text me when you get home," Marcel decided to say.

"I will." It was a promise that Minni could actually keep.

They talked for a few more minutes, but then he had to get back to work and she had a report that wouldn't write itself.

Minni used nearly all of the legal pad, her handwriting neat enough. She handed it back to Longtree who thanked her and happily sent her on her way. Ryan waited for her on the bench in the lobby.

"You gave your statement?" Minni asked as she flopped down beside him.

"Yeah, there wasn't much to it." Ryan shrugged. "Just mostly about hanging around and figuring out the desk drawer had been jimmied."

"Did you see Phil before he left?"

"He said we could go back to New York when we were done. Unless you think there is a reason to stay?"

Minni mulled over that for a moment. "No, I think we're okay. I mean, unless someone else died since we've written our reports?"

The two of them looked at each other, the off the cuff question hitting more seriously than Minni had expected. Minni then asked the receptionist if there had indeed been any more 'events' but apparently it had quieted down.

"I, ah, guess we should go then," Minni told Ryan. He used a pocket sender to message Phil while she texted her uncle, who simply replied to have a safe trip.

It did seem a little weird as they made the very short trek back to the Fort. The moon dominated the landscape as it hung low in the sky. It hadn't gone red yet, but it reflected in snow that was barely disturbed. Almost no one was out this late (or well, early), not in a town like Rome. It was surreal to think that so much death had occurred, both that night and in the past.

They reached Fort Stanwick and retraced their steps to get to the small hut that housed the Shadow Gate. Ryan slipped through first and Minni was left alone in the quiet cold for a moment.

She thought leaving would be more impactful.

That there would be more a sense of dramatic closure. But there wasn't any, not really. The Blakeley's, Phil and Henry, the police… this was just the start of the next act for them. Minni had done her part, had revealed a murderer—several apparently—and now the rest was left for the others to sort out. She might say she left a storm in her wake, but it had already been brewing when she got there.

Minni stepped through the Shadow Gate and met up with Ryan inside the Shadow Realm.

"I swear it's colder in here," Phil groused.

"I have a feeling you could be standing on a beach in the Caribbean on the summer solstice and still be cold." Minni laid her hand on his shoulder, sending some thermal heat through his clothes.

They set off. The walk back seemed like it was longer, as if the Shadow Realm had a renovation in the past few hours and lengthened the paths. Although an actual possibility, it was highly unlikely.

Minni...

Her head shot up and she glanced around. She had already forgotten about the voice, the one which spoke to Canton and egged him into trying to destroy everything. It had tried to lure her off the path when she passed through earlier in what seemed like ages ago.

And now it knew her name.

Minni...

"Everything okay?" Ryan asked after Minni stopped.

"I'm gonna go with a no," she answered, doing a slow three-sixty to make sure nothing was close enough to do them harm. "We stay on the path and we'll be fine."

They kicked up their pace. The path was safe but after the night they had, they didn't want to risk getting dragged into anything. She'd deal with the voice after she had time to discuss it with Phil and see what her options were, if any. They got to the end without incident and exited out into the courtyard.

Minni left Ryan at the Mercury Shop, then stood on the sidewalk trying to decide where to go. Marcel's was closer, but he was at work so his apartment would be empty. Her feet took her on a walk, then on a subway, and she ended up outside Marcel's apartment building. She climbed up the stairs and took out her key. It was probably better if they moved in together at this point. Marcel lived alone, but in less than half the space Minni had, and she already didn't have a lot as New York City standards go.

Letting herself in, she sighed as she took in the familiarity of the place. The tingle of the very light ward she had placed on his apartment, without his knowledge, to keep him a little safer than he might otherwise be. Maybe it was time to... do what? Tell him the truth about magic? Or not, and just hope she could hide it from him if they lived together?

Minni let out an involuntary yawn. She was too exhausted to be thinking about these things right now. This was usually about the time she would start making rash decisions that may or may not work out for her.

She crawled into bed, a couple hours of sleep were better than nothing. She still had to go to work later and the less she used her magic, the better. After the night she had, she could really use Marcel's comfort. But she told him to stay at work--she didn't want him to get in trouble on her account. So she buried her head in his pillow and breathed in his scent.

Like new pennies.

She always knew, she didn't need a werewolf to tell her.

Minni's hand felt paper, a sticky note having fallen from the pillow.

Peek-a-boo it said in Marcel's handwriting.

"I see you," Minni whispered.

TWENTY ONE[21]

August 16th, 2014

Minni probably should have been keeping an eye on them; she was their guide after all. But she'd learned that with wizards, it was best to just let them do their thing and simply keep them from overloading any nearby electronics. They were adults. If they had questions, they'd ask. Usually. Occasionally.

No one had died or been severely injured yet, so…

"Do you have any plans for tomorrow?" Stacey texted her.

"Not at this time," Minni replied.

"Okay, cause I need a dummy." Sometimes Stacey would use her as a live dress dummy so she could work on her tailoring skills. Minni didn't mind. It was actually kind of fun. It made her feel fancy, especially after they broke out the wine.

Minni was debating which emoji she should use in return whilst following the tour group into the next room. There was a big standee about some part of the human anatomy and she gravitated towards it. She'd learned a long time ago that if you hover next to something, you're less likely to get run into or to be blocking the flow of traffic. Especially as her attention was on her phone and not the people around her.

"Peek-a-boo!" A man jumped out from the side, staring straight at Minni's mid-section.

Normally Minni would reflexively reach for her magic when she was startled, and while yes she was caught unawares, frightened she was not. She couldn't tell you why her usual paranoia didn't kick in: only that, in that particular moment, she felt safe.

He glanced up quickly. "You're not Rhianna."

"I'm disappointed too," Minni replied, but the man was already moving past her.

She watched as he searched around the next display only to come out with a child of about ten squealing in delight. He flipped her over his shoulder before setting her back down again. The little girl, Rhianna, ran to the next set of exhibits and the man dutifully followed.

The group of tourist wizards also headed that way, having exhausted their interest in human physiology. Minni went with them as they wandered among a discussion of the cognitive abilities of animals. Her eyes caught on Rhianna, who was very much interested in a display about a parrot. She asked a lot of questions, and the man did his best to answer, usually by reading the information written on the display. He didn't seem annoyed, just very patient.

Minni got pulled along and lost sight of them. She travelled through more exhibits and they eventually ended up in the Great Hall. The inlaid glass in the brick walls created a very ethereal effect as daylight passed through them. Her charges started to argue over what kind of magic spell it most resembled.

"Hey." The man from before stopped next to her as the girl ran forward to look at the current display. "Apologies, about earlier," he said with an easy smile.

"No worries." Minni shrugged, then gestured to Rhianna. "Cute kid."

"Thanks, my cousin's girl." He looked at her proudly. "He's in the hospital right now, so I'm on babysitting duty."

"She seems to be enjoying herself."

"Girl loves science," he commented, then frowned a little. "She was complaining that she doesn't get enough of this at her school, so here we are."

"That's sweet of you. Tell her to remember you when she's the first person on Mars." Minni winked, referencing a previous display in the other building.

He laughed then turned his attention back to Rhianna for a moment. They stood there in easy silence as he watched his cousin and Minni waited for her charges to move on. Minni's phone buzzed in her pocket, but she ignored it.

"I'm Marcel, by the way," he said, glancing at her.

"Minni," she replied.

"So you're a tour guide?" Marcel gestured towards the badge and lanyard Minni wore.

Minni grabbed the badge and looked at it by habit. On the front of it was Minni's photo and the information regarding her employer, Mystical Moments Tour & Travel. Embedded between the two sheets of laminated plastic was very thin copper wire laid out in Minni's sigil. It was basically an extender of her magic-sink properties. The tourists had on similar generic badges.

"More like babysitter," Minni mused. "Most of the tourists want to be left relatively alone. They just appreciate having a local who can answer questions and keep them on schedule."

"Hope they tip well," he laughed.

Minni waited for the inevitable question: You don't sound like a local, where are you from?

The question never came.

Minni answered, belatedly, "I get a good commission."

Rhianna ran up to Marcel and grabbed his hand. "Can we play the mini golf now?"

"Okay," he said, "but no crying when I beat you."

"Please," Rhianna scoffed at him.

Marcel mouthed the words 'I am a goner' as she dragged him out of the room. The Hall of Science had their own mini golf course so he would meet his demise very soon.

Remembering she had a text, Minni grabbed her phone and replied to Stacey. *"2pm is fine."* Then after sending the message, she stared at her phone for a solid five minutes before texting. *"I am an idiot."*

"This has been established," Stacey replied. *"What's up?"*

"Met this cute guy and I dunno, he was just…" Minni started to text but became frustrated. Why was she suddenly angry with herself for not trying to talk to him more? It wasn't even like he flirted with her or anything. He could have a girlfriend or boyfriend and she just… Minni deleted the text and instead wrote. *"I'll explain later. Nothing is on fire so there's that at least."*

Her charges were now finished with the Great Hall and so their time at the Hall of Science was up. They headed back to the entrance, where the mini golf also happened to be situated. Marcel and Rhianna were waiting to go in.

"Hey." Marcel smiled at her. "You wanna join us?" He glanced past her to see the tour group, realizing that she was stuck with them. "Uh, all of you?"

Minni was very tempted, glancing hopefully at the lead wizard who was completely disinterested and very close to leaving without her. "Sorry, they want to go to see the Unisphere. It's not very far from here in Flushing Meadows Park, which you probably already knew…" She trailed off awkwardly.

"My loss then." He smiled softly, then squinted at her as he leaned slightly forward.

"What?"

"I just noticed you had two different colors in your irises," he said, pulling back. "Sorry, it's really pretty interesting."

"Thanks," Minni mumbled. Was he flirting with her or just being nice or…? Minni fumbled with her phone, opening up the address book. She passed it over to him and managed to say, "Maybe we can golf some other time."

She inwardly cringed, but he quickly typed in his number and handed it back to her, meeting her eyes.

"Miss Masterson!" The wizard leader had finally reached the end of his patience.

"I'll text you," Minni said and quickly walked away, not completely sure what just happened.

"That is so unlike you," Stacey said later when they met up. "You never get men's numbers and you never give out yours."

"I know." Minni sat in the common area of the shared apartment she once lived in, trying to sink further into the sofa.

Stacey nudged her foot with her own. "You're gonna text him though, right?"

"Uh, no." Minni laughed nervously.

"Why not?"

"I dunno, he…" Minni was going to say a lot of things, like maybe he was already dating someone, but none of it seemed to fit. Every vibe he gave off told her he was exactly what he said he was. But there was no such thing as a good person; that's what the knight said…

"You're just angry at yourself because you can't find a reasonably good excuse not to text him," Stacey pointed out, giving Minni a not-very-impressed expression.

Minni glared at her, but it had no impact on the woman.

"Ugh, fine." Minni picked up her phone and started a new text. She paused. She didn't know what to write at first.

Should she start with her name?

Remind him that she's the girl from the Hall of Science?

Maybe straight out ask him if he wants to go get drinks or play mini golf?

"Minni…" Stacey gently urged her.

Minni did what she always did and wrote the first thing that came to her mind. *"Peek-a-boo."*

About eight minutes later, she got a return text. *"I see you."*

Then immediately a second text. *"And that sounded less stalkery in my head."*

Minni let out a bark of laughter and covered her mouth. She wasn't sure yet what to make of this Marcel. Handsome and sweet, the way he was patient with his ten-year-old cousin. Perceptive, too. He noticed her eyes, which meant he was actually looked at her and not necessarily just the other areas of her body. There was still a lot she didn't know about him, but at the moment he was seemingly perfect.

Except he was normal.

No magic in him whatsoever.

She had dated non-magic users before, and always seemed to butt up against some issues in not letting it slip that magic is an actual thing that people can do. The greatest trick wizards ever performed was convincing the world that magic didn't exist.

"Is that offer for a round of Mini-Golf still open?" Minni sent back.

It was just one date. What could it hurt?

ABOUT THE AUTHOR

Jessica D. Coplen is a born and raised Oklahoman who loves to travel and learn new things. She received a Bachelor's in History from Northeastern State University in Tahlequah, Oklahoma. She lived in England for several years after college before returning to Oklahoma.

As it is currently the year 2020, she does her part to help protect those around her by staying home or wearing a mask when she has to leave. She's trying to learn how to bake, but, like physics, cooking is basically magic.

Heading into the new year, she remembers Alexandre Dumas who wrote:
"all human wisdom is summed up in these two words,
Wait and Hope."

Special Sneak Peek
Book Four

Copper and Palladium

Copper and Palladium

I was rudely awakened by my phone going off. It wasn't Marcel's ring tone, or the Mercury Shop's, or Stacey. Although I don't know why I thought she'd be calling me when she was curled up at the head of the bed. Point is, it wasn't someone with a set ringtone, so I didn't bother looking. I just cracked one eye open enough to swipe decline.

The phone rang, again.

I declined it, again.

The phone rang a third time.

I chucked it at the wall, missed, and the phone went sailing through the open door into the common area.

"You're gonna break it," Stacey mumbled at me.

"It's shatterproof," I mumbled back. "And waterproof."

"Are you sure about that?"

"I dunno, that's what the dragon said." I momentarily forgot she knows nothing of magic.

"If a dragon sold you a phone and it wasn't solid gold, then what's the point?" Stacey rolled over and buried her head in the pillow. She had a valid point.

Well, I was awake now, or a close proximity thereof. I climbed off the bed, grabbed a small gym bag sitting next to the door, and made my way out into the common area. I may have also kicked my phone and sent it spinning into the kitchen area as I stumbled my way to the bathroom Stacey shared with Gilly.

I did my business and was washing my hands, splashing water on my face, when it happened. The mirror above the sink started to fog over, as if a hot breath had been blown across it. A ghostly hand started to draw letters, slowly and methodically. Lines of water streaked through the words.

This was going to take a few minutes. I reached into the gym bag and grabbed my overnight kit, brushing my teeth as I waited for the message to finish. Someone was trying to get ahold of me via a sending spell. Since I didn't have my sender on me-- well, oops--you know how all those ghosts writing messages on mirrors stories got started? Our bad!

Though I admit I didn't put it together that the person sending me a message might be same person who had been calling me because, well, witches and wizards can't use electronics. Except for me. I can manipulate magic and electricity. I'm pretty much a magic sink. Of the heat sink variety, not the kitchen. Although, some days, an argument could be made…

Minni Masterson! Answer! Your! Phone! – A.D.

My first thought upon seeing the initials was Arthur Dickerson, one of my coworkers at the engineering firm I nine-to-five. But that didn't make any sense because Arthur wasn't a wizard, not even a Forsaken. And he would have no reason to contact me. We don't work on the same projects.

Then my second guess was Avery Dennison. Which made even less sense. How much had I had to drink? I mean, I was barely tipsy when we got back from *Club Paradiso*, but after that…

Eventually, it came to me: Aiden Drake.

And who is this Aiden Drake, other than CEO of Pennington-Kettering Enterprises and honest-to-god real-life gold dragon? He's an asshole, that's who he is. Which is actually an upgrade from a fucking asshole, so there you go.

If that man wanted to speak to me, he could wait.

I smelt like booze and sweat, but I knew that was going to happen; hence the overnight bag. A quick rinse in the shower fixed that right up, along with a change of clothes. I wiped the towel across the mirror, getting rid of the message.

Then, and only then, did I consider taking his call.

I opened the door to see Gilly standing there with an ice cold bottled frappuccino pressed to her forehead. "Please make the ringing stop."

Yeah, I probably should have been more considerate and thought of the other people in the apartment. I realized that after the fact.

"Sorry about that." I set my bag down outside the door and went into the kitchen area. The phone started to ring again and I located it in front of the stove. This time I bothered to look at the caller ID and it was, indeed, Aiden Drake. I took a deep breath before hitting accept. "Listen, Drake. I told you I didn't want to ever talk to you again unless something was literally on fire, so this *better* be good."

Drake only said three words. "Lucy is missing."